D0842187

Let America.

104

McKenzie's Boots

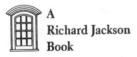

A
Richard Jackson
Book

McKenzie's Boots

MICHAEL NOONAN

ORCHARD BOOKS   NEW YORK
A division of Franklin Watts, Inc.

First published 1987 by University of Queensland Press

Orchard Books, 387 Park Avenue South, New York,
New York 10016

Orchard Books Canada, 20 Torbay Road, Markham,
Ontario 23P 1G6

Orchard Books is a division of Franklin Watts, Inc.

Manufactured in the United States of America
Book design by Mina Greenstein
10 9 8 7 6 5 4 3 2 1
The text of this book is set in 11 pt. Electra.
The characters and events in this story are fictional, but the
times and backgrounds are as they were.

Library of Congress Cataloging-in-Publication Data
Noonan, Michael. McKenzie's boots.
Summary: To escape an unhappy situation at home,
fourteen-year-old Rod McKenzie, six feet tall and more than 154
pounds, enlists in the army during World War II claiming to be
nineteen.   1. World War 1939–1945—Juvenile Fiction.
[1. World War, 1939–1945—
Fiction.   2. Australia—Fiction] I. Title.
PZ7.N75Mc   1988   [Fic]   87–25031
ISBN 0–531–05748–8   ISBN 0–531–08348–9 (lib. bdg.)

TO ROBIN

Prologue

Nelson James Bates had fulfilled an ambition to own a handsome house with a commanding view of Sydney Harbor, one of the most beautiful panoramas in the world. It was an ambition shared with very many more than those who had managed to achieve it, although behind his particular desire was an element shared with no one else. It was partly because a close friend had lived with a sheaf of harbor views crammed into his head like highly illuminated postcards, and had seen it when it had been the setting for great ships, the like of which had never dropped anchor here since.

Now that he was sixty-five and a grandfather five times over, N.J. Bates was still known to his friends—and by some of his many employees—as Nugget, not an unusual nickname, one that had been given to him because of his thick glossy black hair. He still possessed a good head of hair, but it was silver and going white. He had always been nuggety in build, too, and now was shorter but thicker.

From the patio of the Cremorne Point home, a vintage stone residence expensively renovated, he stood and watched an incoming freighter slip past, a modern roll-on, roll-off vessel, brick-colored, with the brand name of a leading Japanese vehicle manufacturer in bold white letters on its side. He checked the time on his wrist from a pricey digital purchased on his last business trip to Tokyo. No doubt about the Japanese. Despite the distance, tides, and weather, right on the dot. After following the freighter's progress upstream for some minutes, he turned and stepped into the spacious lounge adjoining the dining room where his wife had already set the table with linen, silver, and china for a dinner party.

The ship had a link with him in that many of the vehicles it carried would be driven ashore and delivered to his showrooms for sale. After starting out as a mechanic, then acquiring his own garage and expanding into a string of service stations, he owed much of his success to marketing franchises for Japanese motorcars, trucks, and motorcycles. Trophies acknowledging his achievements in this field were on display in the lounge in the form of silver cups, shields, and framed testimonials. Elsewhere on the walls were pictures, some in embroidered silk, of oriental design. One of them, a tiny scene made from the wings of a butterfly, shone like a jewel.

Among the trophies on the sideboard was an altogether different item. A glass case containing a very large pair of brown Australian army boots in what appeared to be good condition, except that the toe-cap of each boot was scored with cuts, mutilations in the style of a crude form of oriental script.

Part One

1

The air was very still that morning, nothing stirred, not a scrap of old newspaper in the gutters, not a leaf overhead, yet the outsize boy who moved so swiftly along the streets and across the intersections might well have had a strong following wind to help carry him forward, propelling him faster than his pounding bare feet could possibly have borne him on their own.

Drivers of trams, buses, vans, taxis, and private cars were startled, even horrified, as he darted across their paths, pausing momentarily on traffic islands, then racing on again, ducking under the outstretched arm of a policeman wrestling with peak-hour traffic, leaving him fuming in a fog of fumes.

Pedestrians stepped hastily to one side as the young runner came weaving toward them. Those he swept past pulled up in alarm and checked back over their shoulders to see if he was being pursued. But he raced alone. To some he gave the impression of being a fugitive; to others that he was involved in some mission of the greatest urgency and importance.

It was apparent at a glance that either he had grown out of his gray serge shorts or that they were much too small for him. A worn leather schoolbag hung over his right shoulder, and he had to keep putting a hand on it to stop it from bouncing on his left thigh and upsetting his balance. He was raw-boned with muscular legs and arms, brown shaggy hair, and in the measurements of the day he was already over six feet tall. His breath rasped, and his face was a high color from the exertion. He appeared to be a schoolboy, but a thick neck, a flattened nose, and skin which had an older texture all contributed to the impression that he might be a youth well in his teens masquerading as a schoolboy.

As he approached and passed Central Railway Station he had clear views of three of the four clock faces on the Latinate tower, all for once, despite their reputation for being out of step with one another, telling the same time. He had half an hour to carry out his mission and be back at Ultimo and in the school grounds for the first bell of the day.

The air was heavy with the smell of boiling hops as he came opposite the soaring brick cliff that walled off one of Sydney's famous breweries. He turned into Elizabeth Street and passed within sight of the high sign of the Tivoli theater where it was reported that ravishing show girls in a touring American extravaganza had appeared wearing only gold paint.

Reaching Hyde Park, he ran on the grass, giving the soles of his feet a respite from the concrete and tar-sealed roadways and pavements. He breezed past the Anzac War Memorial, the noble edifice erected to commemorate sacrifices made in an earlier war, now also serving as a monument to those recently lost in ships sunk by German raiders, U-boats, and mines, and in aerial patrols and dogfights over Europe.

Coming abreast of St. Mary's Cathedral, which he always saw as a sort of stranded sandstone ark, he dodged through the traffic again, then skirted around the sanctuary end of the cathedral and headed into the Domain where there was more cushioning grass underfoot, strewn with the autumn leaves of April 1941.

His run, which was not the first he had made along this route, had begun after coming face to face with the milk carter, Horrie Benson, on a street corner in the inner suburb of Ultimo. On this particular morning, Rod had left for school much earlier than necessary, the reason being that his mother was in a contrary mood after having been sacked the day before from her factory job.

Horrie was on his way home after working through the night and early morning, still in khaki overalls, short-sleeved white singlet, and boots stained gray with splashed milk. Most times when in this attire he emanated a smell of sour milk, and now it was pungent as they met outside the corner pub, where all the bar doors were open as the cellarman hosed the steps and footpath.

"Pity you wasn't with me on the round last night," Horrie began.

"You didn't ask me," Rod retorted, his voice, which had settled deep down in his chest after breaking, momentarily squawking on a higher note. Rod had never been known to turn down any chance to earn some pocket money by helping Horrie lump the cans and deliver the milk and cream.

Grinning at the pained protest, Horrie went on, "You'll never guess what's dropped anchor in the middle of the harbor."

A ship, of course. But what ship? Another big liner? A

battleship? Even an aircraft carrier? Horrie knew Rod's passion for the giants of the ocean-going cavalcade, and now he saw that the boy was plunged into a ferment of excitement and curiosity.

Rod begged Horrie not to tease him by holding out on him. "Aw, come on, Horrie—don't muck me around!"

"Sorry," said the milk carter, shaking his head, which was bald except for a fair wisp of the kind found on babies in prams. "That's somethin' you'll have to find out for your own young self."

"Horrie—please!"

But Horrie was pointing across the street to a hoarding, one showing a ship going down at sea, only its angled stern and twin screws visible above the waves. Horrie repeated its warning words: " 'Don't Talk—the Enemy Listens.' "

At the same time Horrie was wary of the owner of the leg he was trying to pull. The kid had grown so much that he didn't know his own strength: only a week ago, after a quip by Horrie about Rod's increasing size, a friendly push from the victim of his wit had landed the milk carter on his back on the footpath—and Horrie was a six-footer himself.

Horrie put a finger to his lips. "Can't say nothin'—I could be arrested."

Rod was aware of an altogether different ground on which Horrie risked arrest. In the small lunch case, in which the milk carter carried sandwiches, cake, an apple and a banana to see him through the night, there would now be two or three small bottles of purloined cream, all destined to be handed over to the licensee of the corner pub who turned on the beer solely for Horrie before the legal opening time, so that the weary worker could have a few amber nightcaps.

Seizing Horrie's wrist, Rod checked the time. Dried milk

blurred the glass of Horrie's wristwatch, but not enough to obscure the positions of the hour and minute hands. He dropped Horrie's wrist and set off.

As he approached the site of the Art Gallery, Rod was suddenly faced with the sort of dilemma that had left him with a broken and squashed nose.

A squad of soldiers carrying loaded packs were on a training jog from Victoria Barracks, Paddington, and Rod was in danger of running bang into the middle of them. Which way should he veer? Farther out into the Domain grass or right on to the roadway? For no conscious reason he swung left into the Domain, but threw himself off-balance and toppled, sprawling in a tangle of legs, arms, and schoolbag. The soldiers cheered and jeered as they doubled past, their sergeant shouting: "Hup, hup! Unn, doo, tree, taw! Hup, hup!"

Not that the soldiers' derision worried Rod all that much. His tumble was just another example of what he wryly accepted about himself, a rare talent for monumental awkwardness. But at least it hadn't left him damaged. Not like the time he was on an errand to the shops for his mother. He rounded a corner at high speed in bare feet and found the footpath occupied by a small crowd of ladies who had been attending a church social gathering. The traffic was heavy on the road. Rod tried to steer a passage between the two hazards along the concrete edge of the footpath, only to run nose-first into another obstruction in the form of a very solid wooden lamp-post.

He picked himself up from the grass and set his schoolbag over his left hip again and continued to run. Seeing the soldiers had started him thinking along familiar lines, wishing he was old enough to be able to enlist.

It wasn't the uniform that attracted him. Nor was it any so-called glamor attached to it. Not yet. Nor the shine that girls were said to take to anyone wearing it. Not that yet, either. Nor any patriotic urge to support the Empire in its allegedly honorable war against the oppressions of Germany and Italy. It was, quite simply, if one was to try to put into a nutshell those man-made marvels which called for the sweep of ocean seascapes and the settings of great harbors to show them off in all their majesty, the ships—the big ships.

Commandeered and converted from luxury liners to troop transports, their grandeur impossible to conceal under wartime coats of gray, they slipped into Sydney Harbor unheralded, any whisper of their presence forbidden, any mention whatsoever in newspapers banned. They moored at Woolloomooloo, over which Rod now looked as he pressed on along Mrs. Macquarie's Road, and at Circular Quay and in historic Sydney Cove, and on the other side of the Harbor Bridge. They loaded stores, fuel, and military equipment. Troops boarded them from lorries, trains, lighters, and ferries, and then the ships departed under sealed orders, steaming on secret routes for secret destinations.

Despite the indignities they seemed to have suffered, in Rod's eyes they remained floating cities, launched with pomp, ceremony, bands, and champagne. He did not envisage himself ever being able to afford a trip on one of them out of his own pocket, but if he could join the army he might have such a trip at his country's expense. Perhaps on the stately four-funneled veteran *Aquitania*. Better still, on the *Mauretania*, with its squat raked funnels, pressed into service after only a short spell on the Blue Riband route for millionaires across the Atlantic. Infinitely better still, the *Queen Mary*, the world's biggest ship until the French *Nor-*

mandie took the title; and it was the former of these two he believed he started to glimpse as he followed the road which led to the point where he would obtain a sweeping view of the harbor scene that had become his favorite escape from the claustrophobia and grime of Ultimo.

These first glimpses of the massive gray shape anchored out from the convict-built fort, Pinchgut, were through spaces between the wide-branched Moreton Bay fig trees which lined the roadway. A ship more than twice the size of any other to have entered the harbor, truly one of the world's wonders, a holder of the Atlantic Blue Riband, 81,237 gross tonnage, 1,019 feet in length, figures Rod knew off by heart because they were printed on his own model *Queen Mary*. He reached the point where ancient rocks form what an early Governor's wife, Mrs. Macquarie, called her "chair," and from this headland he gazed across rippling water as he feasted his eyes once again on what he believed was now the third biggest ship ever launched. It was the size of such ships that gave Rod a certain affinity with them. There were times when they were so cumbersome that they could not cope on their own; they needed tugs to guide them to their anchorages—something he often felt in need of himself.

As always when he found the *Queen Mary* anchored here, he compared it with another world wonder, the Sydney Harbor Bridge, which loomed to his left. It, too, was painted gray, and, as Rod understood the situation, teams of full-time painters took years to give it a single new coat. If that were so, what a huge task it must be to give the *Queen Mary* such a coat. By making a comparison on this basis, he obtained a measure of the ship's immense size.

But where was the ship Horrie had teased him about?

Rod looked around swiftly, scanning all visible parts of

the harbor for some sign of it—bays and inlets, some crowded with moored yachts and launches, others full of sunlight and shadow. After sighting nothing of significance, he came back to the anchored giant—and then underwent a massive shock.

Instead of having three funnels it had only two.

In his first wild mental gropings for an explanation for this change, he wondered if one of the funnels had been removed to help disguise the ship before it left with the next convoy—only to realize that he was not in fact looking at the *Queen Mary* but at her younger sister, the *Queen Elizabeth*, which had never carried more than two funnels since having been launched after the outbreak of the war. Over two thousand tons and twelve feet longer than her older sister, not only the largest passenger liner afloat but the largest ever.

Wait till the kids at school heard about this! Rod kept appraising the second *Queen*, which he knew to have an extra deck, thirteen in all, seeking and finding certain differences in shape and structure. From one point on its side poured a stream of white water, a torrent large as a waterfall. To his right was a clock face, on a turret among the buildings crowded on the Garden Island naval base. But he remained oblivious to it—until a tender pulling away from a lighter at the *Queen Elizabeth*'s side sprouted a thick plume of steam from its pipe-like funnel and released a sharp whistle which moments later reached Rod's ears like an alarm, reminding him of how little time he had to get back to Ultimo.

As he started running again, he realized that he was in a losing race, something the clock faces of the Central Railway Station tower confirmed.

The clock on the wall of the history classroom showed 9:10 as Rod tried to creep in unseen by the master taking the first lesson of the day, the soles of his feet feeling so raw that he tried to carry his weight on their outer edges.

The master, the formidable Dennis Hillyard, was writing on the blackboard, his back to the class of thirty-five girls and boys, so Rod might well have reached his desk without being caught, except that he stumbled and tried to stop himself from falling by grabbing at a fellow pupil, a desperate maneuver which brought a wail of dismay from the boy seized upon.

Hillyard whirled around from the dates he had been printing on the blackboard. Rod found himself well and truly trapped.

"Murray! You're late."

"I'm sorry, sir." Rod started to slide into the seat of his desk.

"Stand up!"

So Rod kept standing, towering above his fellow pupils, not only because he was on his feet but also because he was so much bigger than them. Older-looking, too. Despite this, like most of the others, he was only fourteen.

Hillyard had a high-powered glare, even though it emanated from small pale-blue eyes. His hair was closely trimmed over the top of his skull, giving him an appearance which had inspired a young bestower of nicknames to call him Prickle-head. Now that hair seemed to be standing up more sharply than ever, as if each strand had somehow become an indignant exclamation mark.

"And what, if indeed any, excuse have you to offer?"

"Well, sir . . ." Rod began. His feet ached, but he writhed more from the discomfort of his situation.

"Did the horse bolt again?"

The class laughed at Hillyard's sarcastic reference to an earlier excuse offered by Rod after Horrie's horse had taken fright at a blast from a motorcar horn and bolted, overturning the cart and spilling out so much milk that they had to call back at the depot to make up the supply.

"No, sir," Rod replied. "I wasn't working last night. You see, sir . . ." He hesitated, overcome with the wonder of it all, before blurting out the amazing news. "It's the *Queen Elizabeth*, sir. She's in the harbor—she's sort of taken the place of the *Queen Mary*."

The response from the class as a whole was the unbridled excitement Rod had anticipated, and for some moments there was pandemonium with much the same question coming at him from all directions: what had happened to the *Queen Mary*?

Hillyard's response was a shouted, "Silence!" He had to repeat himself with a louder shout to restore order.

"I take it," he said to Rod in one of his steeliest voices, as if he might have had a packet of them, like needles, and had selected one of the sharpest, "that you are referring to an ocean liner of that name?"

"Yes, sir. Like I said, sir, she's anchored in the harbor. Where the *Queen Mary* was. The *Queen Elizabeth* . . ."

Hillyard abandoned needles for sledgehammers and shouted: "She is *not* anchored in the harbor!"

"But she is, sir—I saw her."

"You have *not* seen her."

"But, sir . . ."

"Such a vessel is *not* there! The class will forget that you have as much as mentioned its name, let alone its alleged presence. Is that understood?"

There was a prompt murmur of grudging assent from the class.

"And you, Murray," the teacher went on, switching to Rod a glare that might well have been coming from a hostile searchlight. "You will stay behind after the last period this afternoon and write fifty lines on the blackboard." He paused, and recalled what he had seen on a poster locally and elsewhere. " 'The Enemy Listens.' Most appropriate. Fifty times."

Instead of proceeding with the scheduled history lesson based on the dates printed on the blackboard—those of the Wars of the Roses—Hillyard lectured the class about the dangers of spreading rumors. All would clearly recall how, shortly before the Christmas holidays break, they had visited an EXHIBITION OF ARTICLES SEIZED FROM FIFTH COLUMNISTS IN SYDNEY at a city arcade in George Street. German Nazi and Italian Fascist members and sympathizers were still undiscovered and secretly armed, operating high-powered radio transmitters. " 'Walls Have Ears,' " he reminded the class, quoting from other posters. " 'Gossip is Sabotage'; 'Gossipers are Traitors.' " Ever since that exhibition, with its incredible display of confiscated weapons and propaganda, Rod had not doubted that the current war was one for freedom in the face of threatened enslavement.

However, as Hillyard spoke of the dangers of idle talk, guarded, cynical, and amused looks were exchanged by a number of the boys as they were reminded that there were rumors abounding about something the schoolmaster himself was said to get up to on the quiet.

Torture and tantalization, physical and mental, were to be Rod's lot in the next period of the day. The class assembled outside on an asphalt square under the happy green eyes of the honey-blonde sports mistress, Mildred Ross. They formed two circles, with the girls outside, for their second to last lesson before the end-of-term school dance. They began with a Progressive Barn Dance. Recorded music, thin and tinny, came from a loudspeaker attached to an outer classroom wall high over the square.

Rod's feet were toughened since they were so often bare, even in winter; but after the treatment they had suffered on his run to Mrs. Macquarie's Point and back, they still felt raw, especially on the hard asphalt. Mildred Ross saw that he was limping.

"I think you'd better sit this out," she said sympathetically, waving him to a playground bench. Shortly after this she came across to him with a jar of salve for him to rub into the soles of his feet.

"We'll have to make sure you're fit for the dance," she said, and added, "although you mightn't be allowed into the hall in bare feet."

He realized that her warning was well meant. "Don't worry, Miss," he reassured her. "I'll be wearing new boots." A few more nights with Horrie and he would have the money.

"You'll be cutting a dash, I'm sure," she said, leaving him with the warmth of a blindingly beautiful smile.

He occupied the playground bench in a curious style, rather like a stuffed dummy, a Guy Fawkes waiting to be enthroned on top of a stack of wood and dry foliage, his legs stiffly outstretched in front of him so that his feet would not be aggravated by contact with the ground.

From this position, he was free to observe his fellow pupils in action, male and female, and it was one of the latter upon whom his attention soon concentrated—Brenda King, looking more pert and pretty than usual in her short-skirted gym outfit of lavender and brown, the school colors, in readiness for a basketball match with a team from another school at the end of the day.

By her offhand attitude toward him at most times, he had been made to feel the romance they had once shared was now an embarrassment to her. He assumed it was partly because her mother had social ambitions for her. Also because of his excessive size for his age and his appalling clumsiness, which he himself treated as being a sort of affliction, like that of the boy who took epileptic fits and the girl who kept wetting her pants. Nevertheless, he could never forget those moments of delight at the junior school when he and Brenda had played busy bees in an annual pageant, their faces, like their costumes, banded with black and yellow. As well as hugging him, something which her part called for, sometimes she kissed him—and those kisses, even though they had come from an exuberant eight-year-old, remained as fresh in his mind as if they were implanted only yesterday.

She used to allow him to carry her schoolbag home, and they had gone on picnics together when the Murrays and the Kings were friends, on free railway passes to the National Park. For a time she used to sit beside him at school, and his main reason for studying and doing his homework so thoroughly was so that Brenda could copy what he had done. Once, in an examination, she had passed only because he had shifted his paper toward her, so that she could copy his answers.

These days, thanks, it seemed, to her mother's pandering and encouragement, and her own willingness to be so treated, she was bossy, superior, very aware of her hazel-eyed, brunette good looks. Blithely overlooking all such traits and shortcomings, Rod stayed blindly devoted. For him she was still the petite busy bee with the gauze wings who had dispersed rehearsed hugs and unrehearsed kisses.

As he watched Brenda dancing, he began to experience

a full charge of the change which he had been undergoing; he seemed to partake of the same sort of satisfaction when observing either ships or girls. The discovery upset his precarious balance, and he made another pathetic exhibition of himself by falling off the playground bench.

After the last period of the day, Rod reported as instructed to the history classroom where Prickle-head Hillyard was marking exercises with savage jabs and slashes of a blue pencil and mutters of "Woeful!" "Lamentable!" "Beyond belief!" He made Rod wait several minutes before deigning to acknowledge his presence.

"Ah, there, Murray—come to do your lines, eh? There's the empty blackboard—get on with it."

"What'll I use, sir?" Rod inquired.

"What'll you use?" Hillyard repeated with scathing incredulity. "Chalk, you nincompoop!"

"Yes, sir, I know that, sir. But what color?"

"What color!"

"The other day, sir, you said there was a shortage and not to use white or yellow. . . ."

Understanding now, Hillyard shoved the cardboard box of mixed sticks over his desk toward Rod. "There would appear to be a glut of scarlet and purple, so you have a choice."

Rod chose an unused scarlet stick.

With his height and long arms, he was able to start at the very top of the blackboard and work his way down. He had completed just two of the lines when Hillyard scraped his chair around to observe his victim's progress—and then leapt up angrily and snatched the chalk from Rod's hand to correct his spelling of "Enime."

Gesturing him to get on with his punishment, Hillyard remained standing at the rear as Rod carefully completed another line.

"Much better," Hillyard said. "Much, much better." But he spoke in a markedly different tone, as if the angry fighting cock had been turned into a cooing pigeon.

Astonished by this totally unexpected change of tone, Rod turned from the blackboard and looked sharply at the teacher, who compounded Rod's surprise and bewilderment by bestowing an approving smile, after which, in the same ingratiating tone, he said, "Keep going, lad—you're doing well."

What the heck's behind all this, Rod wondered as he faced the blackboard again. Then he stiffened at the touch of a hand very lightly cradling his buttock. This time he twisted around, ready to lash out, but Hillyard had raised his hand and used it to give Rod an encouraging pat on the arm. Then, before resuming his chair at the desk, he smiled apologetically, as if the touch on the buttock had been quite inadvertent.

Rod's next "The Enemy Listens" was a shaky one, as he fought to keep an inward grip on his feelings. In terms of the rumors he had heard about Prickle-head on nature walks, and certain boys slipping off into the bush with him, his action seemed to Rod to be a definite try-on.

The scraping of the chalk on the dry blackboard surface set Hillyard's teeth on edge, so he shoved the exercises into his case, clicked it shut, then stood up and left the classroom, saying, "I'll leave you to it, Murray. Fifty lines, mind. And don't get your spelling wrong—or your sums."

The first twenty lines brought Rod down to the bottom of the blackboard, so he started from the top again, using half a stick of chalk, as he had pressed too hard and broken it in two. He had done another few lines when he heard footsteps in the corridor and at first thought it might be Hillyard coming back to check on him, but the steps were lighter and the fair head of Mildred Ross appeared as she looked into the classroom.

" 'The Enemy Listens,' " she said, reading aloud from the blackboard. "What's all that in aid of?"

She showed such concern that he found himself revealing how he had come by his sore feet, although still refraining from mentioning what he had seen in the harbor.

"It wasn't by any chance the *Queen Elizabeth*?" she asked.

Rod answered with a quick nod.

"That's ridiculous. Everyone knows she's there—they were all talking about it in the teachers' room at morning-tea time. I'd give you a hand with your lines, except that might get both of us in trouble." Then, with a touch of softness and a sad shake of her head, she added, "Poor Dennis."

After pondering for a moment on what Rod took to be the reason for this remark, she fluttered her fingertips to him and continued along the corridor. Her lighthearted attitude made the punishment seem much less onerous, so Rod switched to a purple stick of chalk, and in what seemed no time at all he was able to satisfy himself that, like the number of lashes dealt out to the convict ancestors said to have been on his father's side of the family, there were fifty lines on the blackboard—and that the spelling was correct throughout.

━━━━━━

Still doing sums, but now applying them to the financing of a new pair of boots, Rod set off for home along the street which led to the pub corner near the hoarding which had inspired his fifty lines. In his wake, from the school grounds came shrill schoolgirl cheering—and Rod realized that it must be from the basketball match.

Immediately he turned and sprinted back to the school grounds, as if on the way to see another great ship, except this time it was a girl.

2

Rod's home was in a row of dwellings built for railway workers, all set close except for a narrow pathway down one side of each cottage. Ten front doors in different colors, all mostly faded. Halfway between the first and the last, a horse trough stood over the gutter.

It was here that Rod paused on his way home from the school grounds. The water trickled smoothly in and out, keeping a constant level. With rumors of gasoline rationing, more horses were employed, and a few were brought here to drink. A mounted policeman, a rag-and-bone man with a cart, a scrap-metal dealer with a dray. For Rod the horse trough was the nearest substitute for a creek or a pond. Many times it had become a harbor or an ocean, and in its waters he had sailed his model *Queen Mary*. Not in wartime gray, but in its peacetime Cunard White Star livery, red to just above the waterline where a white strip separated it from the black hull, then white superstructure, and yellow funnels topped with black. It had been a birthday present from his grandmother.

In any event he often lingered before entering the cottage,

never quite sure what sort of a reception he was likely to receive. He passed through the gate, frozen open on its rusted hinges, and through the front door, from which almost all the paint had peeled away, and entered the passageway. In the dim light, after the bright sunshine of the street, he unfortunately restaged one of his recurrent blunders by knocking over the stand on which his father's hats still hung. As he stood it upright again and began to replace the hats on the pegs, his mother's voice came from the bathroom at the rear of the cottage.

"Is that you?"

"Yeah!" Rod called back wearily. Who else could it be but him after announcing his homecoming in such a polished style?

"I ran into that old Mrs. Riordan."

Oh my gosh, Rod groaned to himself, so she's found out! Until a few days ago his services to the local aged and infirm had been accepted without question and much appreciated. It was something he had been encouraged to do by his grandmother, who lived outside Parramatta. He guided old ladies across the street and carried their shopping home for them. "Saved me ole legs," one of them would always say. Or: "You're a real gentleman, Rodney, your blood's worth bottlin'." Sometimes he was rewarded with a few coppers, sometimes a silver threepence, occasionally a whole sixpenny piece. But he never helped with the expectation of receiving money; it was enough for him just to be thanked. "Lending a helping hand is a reward in itself," his grandmother had told him. As for Mrs. Riordan, she had always done a lot of deep rummaging in her purse but had never succeeded in actually locating a suitable coin, so his reward from her had almost invariably been: "Never mind. I'll say a prayer for you."

He'd had his doubts whether this had ever happened. Now, when his mother spoke again, he realized he could expect neither prayers nor mercy.

"She had a go at me about you!"

Rod realized why all too well. He had been shooting up so fast that his ability to control his balance had not kept up with his increasing height and lengthening limbs. He had become uncoordinated in a way not only distressing to himself but also dangerous to others.

"She said it was only because she was such a kind, forgiving, Christian woman that she didn't report you to the police."

Provoked into a defense, Rod called back. "All I did was fall over."

"*All!* You fell *on* her!"

"I didn't mean to."

"She said she thought you were going to rape her."

"*Rape* her!"

"That's what she said."

"She's an old lady!"

"So what?"

"And it was broad daylight."

"And you're your father's son."

"What's that got to do with it?"

"Daylight or dark, old ladies or broomsticks, they were all fair game to your dad."

"Mum, I didn't mean any harm. It just happened. I stepped onto something sharp and—well—fell over."

"So you weren't wearing your boots."

As Rod tried not to answer this one, his mother appeared at the far end of the passageway, her head swathed in a towel after washing her hair, a statuesque figure in a close-fitting robe, a woman described as handsome in spite of her bouts of dissipation. She'd had a very bad day, no response anywhere from the factories where she had tried to land a job, even with a manpower shortage building up.

"I asked you a question," she said.

"No," he said. "I wasn't."

"What's the point of me buying you new boots if you don't wear them!"

"They don't fit any more."

"You don't mean you've grown out of them, too!"

"I can't help m'self growing!"

"Put a brick on your head or something."

Or something, he thought, as she turned into her bedroom. They say if you play with yourself too much it stunts your growth.

Calling from within her bedroom, she went on: "I can't do anything about it."

"I'm not asking you to," he called back. "I'm savin' up. And I've nearly got enough."

If his mother made a comment, he did not hear it.

His father, a railway workshops storeman, had enlisted a few days after the recruiting booths opened and had been overseas with the Second AIF for more than a year. Rod had commandeered the footwear he had left behind—boots, shoes, sandshoes, slippers—but had grown out of all of them. Not only these, but his grandfather's, unearthed when going through cupboards at his widowed grandmother's happy little shack.

In contrast to her daughter's attitude, his grandmother took pride in Rod's manly proportions. As she had told him many times, his ancestors were mostly men over six feet tall with big ears (which Rod certainly had) and had served for generations with famous British regiments, and fought in countless famous battles, and had included a great-great-grand-uncle aged sixteen in the Crimean War.

Whether Rod's size was hereditary or not, it had come between him and his mother. He understood and accepted the situation, her predicament and his. When he was smaller, she used to take him in her lap and cuddle him, often breaking down and weeping and saying that his father didn't love her any more and that he was keeping company with strange women. Tom Murray himself became something of a stranger to his family, and it was a relief to his wife when he enlisted. He sailed on the *Orcades* in a convoy with the mighty battleship HMS *Ramilles* heading the naval escort. There had been no word from him since he had embarked. His allotment of two shillings a day kept coming in, however, together with the government daily allowance to his wife, and five shillings a week for his son. Because of her heavy drinking and smoking, this was not enough, so Rod's mother had to work.

A few months after his father left, Rod had found his mother sitting in the front room, forlorn and sad, so he sat in her lap, not so much to be cuddled as in the past; rather to try to offer her some comfort in her misery. She had reacted as if he had physically attacked her, pushing him away and crying out: "You monster! Get off! You're crushing me!"

At that moment, boyhood for Rod had come to an end. Not that he felt he had suddenly stepped across a divide into young adulthood; rather that he had been catapulted into adult territory without enough knowledge of it to be able to find his way. Since that day, there had been no physical contact between mother and son, no touch of affection. A barrier of embarrassment had come between them, one which seemed to incite his mother into suggesting that Rod was somehow responsible for the troubles she had brought upon herself.

He didn't resent this. He simply blamed his size and ineptness, and left it at that—although he kept hoping that his rate of growth might at last be slowing down. To try to gauge this he would cup his hand around his ear, as if turning it into a seashell. Instead of the subdued roar of an ocean, he heard an insistent seething—the sort of sound he imagined might be detected in tropical forests where grasses, vines, and plants were said to burgeon and proliferate with such speed that you could actually hear them growing. From the seething he now heard within the shell of his cupped hand, he could only conclude that much the same thing was still happening to his flesh and bones.

The next morning his feet had recovered and there were only minor twinges from them as he reached the school grounds. One of the boys, the son of a harbor ferry engineer, had the answer to what had happened to the *Queen Mary*. After loading troops, she had gone out to sea and would be joined by the *Queen Elizabeth* as soon as the sister ship had taken her quota of troops on board. Apparently, despite the vaunted vastness of Sydney Harbor, in the event of a gale blowing up when the two *Queens* were anchored, there was not enough room for both of them to swing safely. Another boy had a different version: there might not be enough tugs available to control the two leviathans at the same time.

Rod looked around for Brenda King, but didn't see her until the class was filing into the history room. She was wearing a plain navy tunic and seemed a bit downcast; her basketball team had been badly beaten the previous afternoon. Rod had slipped away from the game, a little fearful that blame for the defeat might somehow be linked to his presence as a spectator. In much the same way as, in the morning, his mother had seemed to imply that he was to blame for the hangover she was suffering following a session after hours at the corner pub with some of her girlfriends.

In the classroom, Rod's fifty scarlet and purple lines were still on the blackboard next to the dates of the Wars of the Roses. One boy started to chant the words "The Enemy Listens" and others took it up in high and low voices, going up and down the scale, until silenced by the arrival of Dennis Hillyard.

He eyed the blackboard and its embellishments sourly. His usual practice was to call on someone other than the writer of the lines to come forward and count them to ensure that the punishment had been correctly carried out. Then he would call upon the victim to remove his or her handiwork with the flat blackboard duster.

He shot a quick glance in Rod's direction, avoiding his eyes, then he departed from his routine by using the fifty lines as the basis for another stern lecture about the dangers of loose talk, and gave the class another summary about how the present conflict had started and how it was progressing. None too well, alas, for those with right on their side. The cities of England were still being bombed by the Luftwaffe, even though the RAF was striking back. The Germans had just invaded Greece, and Australian troops were in the front line.

Hillyard clearly relished such discourses, but to Rod they were flights of phony patriotic fancy. He put Prickle-head on a par with some of the cranks who spoke in the Domain on Sundays.

Most Sunday afternoons, after looking over the harbor and its ships, Rod wandered through the Domain. He had been impressed by the sincerity of a white-haired, wheezy-voiced battler who stood precariously on top of a set of folding steps and spoke out against all the flag-waving. He quoted a famous man who had claimed that ardent avowals of patriotism were suspect because, too often, they were resorted to by scoundrels. This statement, in Rod's opinion, applied to Hillyard, who concluded the period by taking up the duster and reducing Rod's fifty lines to a flurry of scarlet and purple dust as he removed them from the blackboard. Rod grinned, at the same time aware that Hillyard kept avoiding his eyes; but as he grinned, he noticed that several boys eyed him particularly sharply. All were rumored to have been among those who had slipped away to meet up with Prickle-head in the bush during his nature walks.

In the playground during the mid-morning break, Spider Benson, the eldest of Horrie's scrawny kids, ran across to Rod to pass on a message.

"Dad said can you give him a hand tonight."

Tonight was Thursday; Rod wondered if the milk carter had confused it with Friday, when he almost always helped on the round.

"Tonight and tomorrow night, too," Spider told him.

"Suits me," Rod said. It augured well for his campaign for a new pair of boots.

Before the break ended, Rod was approached by another go-between, Fran King, Brenda's younger sister by a year.

"Our kitchen light-bulb's blown," she told Rod. "Mum said could you drop in and change it for us on your way home?"

Of course, he could. And he did, even though his own mother would be furious if she knew he was doing any more menial tasks for the Kings.

When he called at the King home, all he had to do was

reach up and twist out the dead bulb and then fit the new one. For once his height was of some use, although he didn't get the new bulb in properly the first time he tried and it slipped down and would have hit the kitchen floor and smashed if Fran hadn't caught it. So instead of receiving thanks from Brenda and Mrs. King, he heard a joint groan of relief.

————

A number of aspects of the war pleased Horrie Benson very much. It meant that the milk and ice company which employed him had postponed a plan to switch from horse-drawn carts to motor vehicles. The prospect of having to learn to drive a truck and keep getting in and out of the front seat, starting up and stopping, had not appealed at all. His horse, Edgar, might not be the most handsome animal of his species, but he knew the round by heart and trundled the cart from one stop to the next. So well did he know it that on at least one occasion, after having accepted too much liquid hospitality from a customer, Horrie would have missed an important stop but for Edgar.

The cart was a well-sprung two-wheeler painted a glossy cream and edged with red and gold stripes. It had a high front seat behind a bar to which the reins could be tied, and under the seat were compartments in which Horrie carried bottled cream and kept his lunch box, Thermos flask of hot tea, and a bottle of rum. The main body of the cart was a sort of container for a tank of milk, which had a small lidded manhole at the top and a tap at the rear.

Rod's routine was to go to bed for an hour or two, then walk—or more often run—from Ultimo to the milk and ice company depot in Surry Hills, to be there by ten o'clock.

With Rod alongside Horrie on the front seat, they would start out, giving Edgar his head. He turned left out of the depot, which was in the heart of a run-down slum area. If the lights at the first intersection were red, Edgar stopped until they changed to green. He was meticulous about traffic lights. Once, when they jammed on red, Edgar refused to budge, even though Horrie yelled at him to go, flicked the reins, and would have resorted to using a whip, except that he didn't carry one. Rod was on the round this night and thought Edgar's conduct highly amusing, a sentiment not shared by Horrie, who ordered his offsider to climb down from the seat, take the horse by the bridle and drag him through the red lights. Edgar had one great failing. He had a taste for the canvas hoods of roadsters and tourers, whether up or folded down, and chewed them, old and ultra-modern models being consumed with equal relish.

The milk carter and his offsider crossed the tram tracks at King's Cross and plunged into high society as they serviced the people of fashionable Darlinghurst, Elizabeth Bay, and part of Rushcutters Bay, filling large cans from the tap at the rear of the cart and using metal dippers to transfer the milk to small cans, jugs, and other receptacles with plates and covers over them against marauding cats, ladling out pints and quarts and supplying cream on request. The houses and mansions, some still private residences, and the blocks of flats, were Courts, Lodges, Closes, Halls, Towers, Villas, populated by glamorous people, actors and actresses, artists, writers, poets, musicians, many of whom were known to Horrie by their first names: people as famous as Chips Rafferty, Bill Dobell, Dame Mary Gilmore. Some of the city's leading gangsters lived here in style as well, and according to Horrie were the most generous of men when entertaining at home, however mean and unsavory their reputations.

It was all an adventure to Rod, especially now with the *Queen Elizabeth* anchored in the harbor. Ascending blocks of flats by service elevators or back stairs, from the rooftops he had glimpse after glimpse of the world's biggest ship looking more silver than gray, the water lavender in the night light, with a stream of launches, tenders, and lighters coming and going as over five thousand troops from military camps were taken on board.

To Horrie, these men were "cannon-fodder." He claimed that the volunteers were only interested in escaping from home and their jobs and seeing something of the world for free. Rod agreed with this only to an extent. He accepted that his own father had enlisted mainly to get away from his family and a dreary job; but at the same time, Rod believed that many of the recruits were motivated by a desire to serve their country in a war against the forces of evil.

For Horrie the nightly round was as much a series of social calls as work, stops for cups of tea or coffee, beer, wine, spirits, and what appeared to Rod to be an occasional drenching in strong perfume. Deep in the night, in this sophisticated part of the great city, many were awake and active, not just insomniacs but late partygoers, illegal gamblers, theater and night-club workers, and the lonely to whom the rattle of a milk dipper on a can was enough to make them open their doors and invite Horrie in for a spell.

Such aspects of the milk carter's nocturnal life didn't disturb Rod, even though he knew Horrie's wife, a merry little woman, and his five kids. Rod seemed to have an inbuilt tolerance about such things, and Horrie himself had vouched for where his marital and family fidelity lay, saying, "Of course, if I wanted to get away from the missus and the kids, I'd join up like a shot." Besides, it seemed to Rod that Horrie was providing a sort of charitable service to those in need of company. Surely no harm would come from it—always provided that Edgar wasn't suddenly transformed into a talking horse obsessed with the sins of others, like some of the fire-eaters who fulminated from their soap-box podiums in the Domain on Sunday afternoons. It seemed to Rod that Horrie's socializing was carried out in much the same spirit as his own help to the local old ladies (but since the incident with the devout Mrs. Riordan, his one and only attempt, in this case to assist the arthritic Mrs. Ashworth safely across the street, had met with a horrified raising of gnarled hands and an emphatic "No-thank-you-very-much!")

It was dawn when they completed the round. Edgar knew the way home, and after a final stop at the traffic lights, they were back in the Surry Hills depot by six o'clock. After being paid, Rod headed for home for a couple of hours' sleep before going to school, leaving Horrie to unharness and stable Edgar, then juggle his books and takings before settling with the depot cashier. Rod's basic pay was two shillings, but sometimes Horrie added some loose copper coins.

The next night, starting Friday and going into Saturday, was the biggest round of the week, with many customers leaving out notes for extra milk and cream. Rod calculated that the night's pay, added to the money in his bedroom drawer, meant he would have enough to go shopping for his new pair of boots.

As he didn't need to hurry home to rest before school, at the depot he helped Horrie unharness and stable Edgar. Besides, he needed to consult Horrie about the best places to shop for the boots.

"You could save yourself the dough and borrow an ole pair of mine," Horrie said.

"Thanks all the same," Rod said, anxious not to appear ungrateful. "But I want them for the next school dance." Meaning that he preferred to obtain brand-new boots.

"Please yourself, sport. But those boots have done a lot of dancin' in their time. There was a little red-head in Brockley Court, eighth floor. She liked to start off the evening with a dance or two. Foxtrots and two-steps. Had a wind-up gramophone—and, boy, did she get herself wound up!"

After collecting his two shillings and an extra threepence, Rod left for home, and with the money still in his pants pocket he flopped on his bed. From the next bedroom came his mother's heavy breathing, breaking into flubbers, a sure sign that she had been drinking heavily. Despite this, he was soon asleep himself.

It was nine o'clock when he woke, and the first thing he heard was more of the same heavy breathing from his mother's bedroom. It must have been a really heavy night. He crept past her bedroom door, anxious not to disturb her; if woken she was bound to be in a bad mood. He had two slices of bread and plum jam (the smell of toast might wake her up) and a glass of milk from the free billy-can Horrie allowed him.

He was ready for his buying spree. He crept back to his bedroom and took the two shilling piece and the threepence from his pants pocket; then he opened the drawer where he had left the rest of his nest-egg in one of the ornate tobacco tins which had been his grandfather's. At first he thought he had lifted the wrong tin: it was so much lighter than it should have been. There was no sound when he gave it a quick, alarmed shake—and then, when he opened it, no coins to shake.

He opened the other tobacco tins, but they were empty

too. He shifted things around in the drawer—his collection of cigarette cards, marbles, stamps, miniature motorcars, but there wasn't a copper or silver coin in sight. His first assumption was that they'd had a visit from the burglar Mrs. Riordan claimed had stolen her garnet rosary-beads, which had come from Rome after having been blessed by Pope Pius the XIth. In a mounting frenzy, he dragged out other drawers, wrenched open cupboards, threw socks, shirts, and shorts on the linoleum floor. He knew it was pointless, but he had to do something, even if only to find an outlet for his mortification at his crushing loss. And then he became aware that his mother was standing in the doorway, hair straggly, eyes bleary, mouth gaping, woken out of her stupor by the racket.

Still assuming that he had been the victim of a burglary, Rod picked up the empty tobacco tin and held it out—and then his mother's expression told him who the robber had been.

She let out a wail of remorse and rushed at him, arms outstretched.

"I'm sorry! I'll pay you back!"

Momentarily paralyzed with disbelief, Rod found himself with her arms wrapped around him, her breath fetid with stale gin. As she sobbed piteously, he broke free and ran away from the cottage, outside into the fresh air and along the street. He stopped when he reached the corner pub and stood on the wet pavement just hosed down by the cellarman. He leaned closer to an open bar door and heard voices from behind the tiers of bottled spirits and wines that separated the public and saloon bars. Yes, Horrie was still here. Taking a moment to compose himself, Rod entered the bar at a forced saunter, which meant he walked so stiffly that he nearly slipped on the damp tile floor.

"Out!" the publican said in a gravelly voice. "This pub's not open yet—an', besides, if I'm not mistaken, you're underage." The publican glowered, his eyes rheumy-red, the skin on his face and double chins the texture of sandpaper.

But Horrie was holding up a placatory hand.

"She'll be right, Bert," he said. "What is it, Rod?"

Giving nothing away about what had happened at home, Rod said, "Them old boots of yours."

"Want to borrow 'em?"

"If it's okay with you."

"Sure." Horrie drained his glass. "Thanks, Bert," he said, then nodded to Rod to follow him. "I'll get 'em for you."

As they plodded side by side to the Benson cottage, Horrie asked, "Your mum got a new job yet?"

"Don't know," Rod said, which was the truth—except that he had little doubt the answer was no.

"Thought she mighta done. Bert said she was in last night after-hours with a mob, spending up big."

Rod made no comment.

3

When Horrie produced the old boots, Rod wondered whether he might have done better by going to a rubbish dump or some lonely beach. With a dry gray crusting of splashed milk they looked as if they had been cast in lead.

Being naturally courteous, quite apart from what his grandmother had instilled in him, and genuinely grateful, he expressed his thanks to Horrie, then sat down on the back step of the Benson cottage, surrounded by three of Horrie's kids, as he tried one of the boots for size.

His foot didn't stand a chance of getting into it.

"Gee," Horrie said, "I didn't know you'd grown that much bigger than me."

"Me, neither," Rod said. "But thanks all the same."

"What are you gonna do? Buy a new pair after all?"

"No—not yet."

"I thought you said you had the money."

Horrie had been curious ever since Rod had turned up at the corner pub, because when they parted earlier in the morning Rod had a list of shops to visit. On his part, Rod was aware that his conduct was inconsistent, and he seized on an explanation.

"I decided Mum could have it."

"The money you saved?"

"Yeah."

Horrie now showed real concern. He wanted to talk to Rod alone and waved his kids to clear off.

"You decided your mum could have the money?" Horrie said, just to make sure that he understood what he had just been told.

"Yeah," Rod said again.

"That's one sure way of pissing it down the drain."

Rod still made no comment. Horrie knew him well enough to know he wouldn't get anything more out of him.

"I might be able to help after all. How about a pair of sandals?"

Rod reacted hopefully. "I suppose I could wear them—with socks, of course."

The sandals were also a crusted gray—but when Rod tried them on, they were quite a reasonable fit; it didn't matter that his toes protruded a little at the front.

Whether he would be allowed into the hall for the dance wearing such sandals, even with socks, he didn't know, but he took them home to clean them.

His mother was asleep again, breathing gently. Careful not to run foul of the hat-stand, he started to tip-toe down the passageway, but was in danger of losing his balance and crashing his shoulder against the wall, so he adopted a slow flat-footed walk until he emerged through the back door into the small enclosed yard. A path laid with bricks led to a lean-to where his father had kept a few tools.

Rod used a paint-scraper to remove layers of crusted milk from the sandals. They looked grayer and there was little of the original color left to indicate that they had been brown. Again at great pains not to make any noise, he took the boot-polish box from the scullery, then sat on a bench in the yard and was amazed at how much Nugget the leather absorbed. It responded to vigorous polishing by showing a very mild shine. The sandals now looked reasonably respectable, and he had a pair of plain brown socks that would go with them.

He became so absorbed in his task that he didn't notice the appearance of his mother, who didn't notice him until she was at the door of the outside lavatory.

She burst into tears again and promised that she would pay him back and buy him a handsome new pair of boots and change her errant ways. Rod shrugged; he regarded his nest-egg as having been irretrievably donated to Bert Heffernan's corner pub. And she didn't pay him back. Certainly not in time for the school dance on the eve of the break-up for the May holidays.

If this had been the fancy-dress dance held later in the year, Rod felt he would have been able to go as a scarecrow. The combination of the sandals and stretched socks didn't look too bad, but his only pair of long trousers were now well above his ankles and tight around the crotch and waist. His mother had gone out with some male and female factory friends, who had called in a ramshackle car, so he had only his own opinion about his appearance. After leaving the house, he stopped at the horse-trough, which was very still and reflected the nearby street-lamp, a miniature Atlantic Ocean with its own moon, where Rod had sailed his model *Queen Mary* from Southhampton, England, and Le Havre, France, to New York, U.S.A. Someone he expected to see tonight—indeed, the main reason for his attendance at the dance—had a link with the great liner. Brenda's father had sailed on her in the convoy which took him to the Middle East. Rod had some interesting information about how the first of the *Queens* had been converted into a troop transport, after talking to an engineering apprentice from Cockatoo Shipyards at Mrs. Macquarie's Point one Sunday. He was eager that Brenda should know what he had gleaned, especially as her father had become an officer before sailing, a lieutenant.

The dance was held at the old hall in the school grounds. A man from the Parents' Association was on the door, and he cheerfully waved Rod inside.

The scene dazzled him: colored streamers and balloons hanging from the rafters; the girls in party frocks of satin, silk, and taffeta, ribbons in their hair, shiny patent-leather shoes, eyes bright, many wearing lipstick, rouge, and eyebrow pencil. An ensemble of senior pupils waited to start the music as they sat in a foursome on one side of the stage—piano, violin, clarinet, and drums. On the other side of the stage sat members of the staff and parents—Rod noted that Dennis Hillyard was among the teachers. In fact, it was as if Hillyard had been waiting for him to appear. After having avoided Rod's eyes since before Easter, the schoolmaster was now aggressively seeking a visual confrontation, which Rod found very disturbing. Then the music started, after Mildred Ross, ravishingly beautiful in a long golden lamé evening dress, announced a Progressive Barn Dance.

As the couples changed, Rod found it was his turn to dance with Brenda King, who looked radiant, her slightly pouted lips as succulent as cherries. She wore makeup. Her brown hair shone. Her hazel eyes glowed. And at him, too.

"Thank goodness you're here!" she astonished him by saying, speaking rapidly because couples had so little time together before changing partners. "Mother's gone mad again and wants to shift the furniture. Do you think you could help?"

" 'Course," he said. How could he refuse?

"Tomorrow morning?"

"Okay," he said, and then they were parted.

As the dance finished, still dazzled, he bumped his way through the throng to the end where the boys were gathering. Mildred Ross was a glittering figure up on the stage again, presumably to announce the next dance; but no, it was to say that the headmaster had to leave early but wished to speak first.

He was a gray-haired man in failing health who had postponed his retirement because of a growing shortage of teachers caused by wartime enlistments. He began by thanking everyone for attending the function and wished them a happy night, then went on to announce: "Another valued member of our staff has volunteered and been accepted for service with the A.I.F. We are sorry to see him go, yet we are honored that he should choose to enlist. I speak of Mr. Dennis Hillyard."

The headmaster turned to where Hillyard sat, then led the enthusiastic applause, not wholly to honor the volunteer for his loyalty to his country, but partly to celebrate getting rid of him. All the same, it came as an all-round surprise. No one had imagined Prickle-head joining up; he had established himself as a waver of the flag but not a potential participant, his self-appointed role hitherto having been to urge others to enlist and fight.

Hillyard limited his response to a stiff bow before sitting down again, after which Mildred Ross stepped forward on the stage to tell the dancers to take their partners for a Boston Two-step.

Rod looked to where the girls had bunched themselves apart from the boys. Brenda sat beside her young sister Fran. Buoyed up with courage after his encounter with Brenda in the Progressive Barn Dance, Rod headed straight for her, and instead of saying, "May I have the pleasure of the next dance?" as he and others had been taught by Mildred Ross, he blurted out, "How about it?"

Since she was to be indebted to him for his furniture-moving services, Brenda treated his request as if perfectly framed and smiled and answered, "I'm sorry, I'm booked for this one . . ." something Rod was already realizing as a boy had come to claim her ". . . the next perhaps."

"Sure thing," Rod said, left standing lost and alone, until he became aware that Fran, who was not rated in the same class as her elder sister when it came to good looks, was giving him a friendly smile. But he'd had his mind so set on asking Brenda to dance, it simply didn't occur to him that he could have asked Fran instead.

To rejoin the main body of males, he had to skirt around the dancers. Almost at the male retreat, he found himself blocked by Dennis Hillyard, angry furrows along his brow, eyes glaring.

He spoke partly between his teeth, his face close to Rod's. "It was you who told tales to the headmaster, was it not?"

"Me?" said Rod, staggered and completely baffled. "Me tell the headmaster? I've never ever even spoken to him in my life." And it was a fact that Rod, like many others, had never had any personal contact with the august personage.

"Of course you did," Hillyard insisted. "Out of spite—because I gave you those fifty lines."

Having accused Rod of something which remained un-defined, the teacher pushed past him. He was on his way to the door. Now that the headmaster had announced the valiant step he had taken, he seemed in a hurry to leave the dance, scuttling out in the way which had prompted someone to say that there could be some cockroach in him.

Rod remained utterly mystified until he glanced to one side and saw someone watching him closely. One of the boys who had noticed in the history classroom that Prickle-head was avoiding Rod's eyes; one of the boys said to have been a party to what had gone on when Prickle-head had vanished into the bush with them. Sam Chivers.

Among his grandmother's sayings was: "You need to know how to put two an' two together, Rodney—it'll always stand you in good stead. Your mother never really could."

So he put two and two together and came up with an answer. Chivers had been jealous, and he could have informed the headmaster. Already an explanation for Prickle-head's courageous act was circulating in the hall; the teacher hadn't volunteered willingly, but had been given an ultimatum—either join up or be shown up and booted out of the school.

In the Progressive Barn Dance, Rod had performed competently, his feet comfortable in the socks and sandals, but Hillyard's attack had undermined his confidence, so that when he approached Brenda again, he felt that he had an uncertain control over himself and was liable to perpetrate some gaffe, possibly verbal, but more likely physical.

A bracket of three dances began with a jazz-waltz and Rod was in trouble with his rhythm for a start. He persisted with his intention of telling Brenda what he had found out about the accommodation for officers on the *Queen Mary*, and had great difficulty in speaking and dancing at the same time. What he tried to say was that the best parts of the ship (according to his informant) had been allotted to the officers. The original ornate main dining room was their mess, and they had the prize forward sun deck for recreation and the best cabins. His timing became worse with the quicker second part of the bracket, the foxtrot, and infinitely worse in the still faster two-step. As much as she might like to hear that her father had set off for the war in the sort of luxury millionaire travelers had enjoyed, Brenda could endure only so much of having her feet trampled on.

She gave up the dance and him, saying, "I think I'd better sit down."

He was left to shoulder his way blindly through other two-stepping couples, disgusted with himself for making such a colossal botch of things. At the edge of the dance floor he felt a small hand on his arm and looked down to find Fran at his side.

"I'll dance with you, Rod," she said, gently taking hold of his hands, making them appear inordinately large and hers tiny and delicate in comparison.

Still feeling badly out of kilter, Rod allowed himself to be led by Fran, who managed to restrain herself from wincing when Horrie's sandals stamped on her feet. She even managed an encouraging smile from her up-tilted face and said, "You're not too bad, considering."

This time, it took some moments for Rod to put two and two together, and the question had popped out before he had given himself a chance to decide that it was one which might be better not asked.

"Considering what?"

"Well," she said, putting it in the sweetest way, indeed almost as if it were a claim to distinction, "you have sort of got very big feet. . . ."

As Brenda had abandoned him, Rod left Fran standing on her own, immediately regretting what he had done, yet somehow powerless to have stopped himself from doing it.

He glanced back just once before escaping from the hall, as determinedly as Dennis Hillyard had done; and that glance made it even worse for him, because he saw the look of shock and dismay on Fran's face together with something else he hadn't really noticed before—that she was really very pretty.

———————

Back home, Rod stopped at the horse-trough and dropped bits of broken concrete from the pavement into it, making a series of tidal waves. His mother was at home, the beaten-up tourer parked outside, her friends babbling and laughing raucously in the front room as they drank. Fortunately, the door to the sitting room was almost closed, so he slipped past along the passageway to his bedroom. Once in bed, he lay in the dark, brooding over his failure at the dance, and deciding that he had been badly treated by Brenda and that he certainly would not help move the family furniture the next day, no matter what he might have promised. Her behavior had been unforgivable.

What about his own behavior, though? In terms of his grandmother's gentlemanly aspirations for him, he had let her down—and himself. He heard her voice another of her sayings: "Whatever happens in life, you mustn't hold grudges, you only end up harmin' yourself. You don't have to forget, mind you—but it's always better to forgive."

And so his resentment melted away, and he fell into an easy sleep, waking in the morning ready to call at the King home around the corner in a row of superior cottages, originally constructed for overseers and inspectors.

Before moving there, the Kings had lived a few doors from the Murrays. Rod didn't let on to his mother where he was going. She considered Helen King a snob. In the railway service their husbands had been on exactly the same level as storemen, but now Alec King had found success in the army by becoming an officer, something that vastly increased his wife's social standing.

Fran answered the door when Rod knocked. He blurted out that he was sorry for leaving her stranded at the dance. His appearance here was an apology in itself, and she was understanding.

"I shouldn't have said what I did," she told him.

Hearing their voices, Brenda appeared in the passageway, one which was wider and higher than those in the cottages where Rod and his mother lived. Although momentarily showing relief that he had arrived, she quickly assumed something of the air of affectation encouraged by her mother.

"I was telling mother what you told me last night. About the *Queen Mary*."

"Yes, indeed," said Helen King, appearing and taking over. "Alexander seemed very modest about it in his letters, but I had the feeling he'd been allotted a prime cabin."

Helen King was wearing a two-piece costume and some junk jewelry in readiness to leave for her voluntary war work, helping at a club for officers. She was running late, but outlined Rod's program of work. Brenda and Fran had shared the second bedroom. Now Fran's furniture was being moved to the back room so that each girl could be on her own. Next, she would like the settee and armchairs moved in the drawing room (the front room, known as the sitting room at Rod's place), and after that, she wondered whether Rod might have a look at the back drain, which seemed to be very slow to clear. In other words, it was blocked.

"What's the latest about your father?" she asked, after disappearing briefly to fit on a cloche hat, and drawing on gloves, as worn by well-dressed officers' wives.

"Haven't heard," Rod said.

"I expect by now he's had some promotion."

"Don't know," Rod said. He tended to use his shoulders to help him to reply to such questions, but as he was carrying a wall mirror from Brenda's bedroom to Fran's, he couldn't shrug.

"Alexander's a captain now, so it shouldn't be too long before we hear he's received his majority. I suppose you just can't wait till you're old enough to join up."

She gave him no chance to reply, saying as she went off, "Your mother's lucky to have a strong man about the house."

And so she departed, little realizing what she had done.

Until now it hadn't occurred to Rod to try to join up, simply because the age of enlistment seemed too far off. He certainly had the necessary size. In Brenda's bedroom, a framed photograph of her father in officer's uniform sat on her dressing-table. For the first time Rod began to wonder what he might look like in army uniform. He believed it would undoubtedly enhance his standing in the eyes of the occupant of this bedroom.

Instead of returning the sandals to Horrie, Rod asked if he could borrow them for a little longer—and also a suit and hat (his father's hats on the stand in the cottage passageway were already several sizes too small for him).

"Going for a job, eh?" Horrie said.

"Yeah," Rod answered, truthful in a sense.

"Sure it's not because you're sneakin' out with some girl?"

"Could be," Rod said with a grin.

"Okay. That suit an' hat could do with an airin', the missus says I never take her anywhere. Don't forget, though, there's always a job goin' at the depot if you want it."

Rod knew that and nodded. He had already made up his mind that he wasn't going back to school after the term break. He was over fourteen, in fact in three months he would be fifteen, so legally he could leave. And he didn't think his mother would be much concerned one way or another what he did.

"There'll still be one or two nights a week for you on the round. More if too many of the husbands go off to the war." Horrie rolled his eyes wickedly. "I might have to put you on to a couple of 'em, to help me out. Whaddaya reckon?"

Rod responded with a guarded shrug, and Horrie laughed and slapped him on the shoulder. "Awlright, only pullin' your leg. I know your next'll be your first."

This time Rod neither nodded nor shrugged. He didn't particularly want to expose himself by agreeing; nor did he want Horrie (or anyone else for that matter) thinking he wasn't interested.

Rod collected the suit, a brown double-breaster, and the hat, also brown, took them home and put them in his bedroom wardrobe. After his reaction to the disappearance of his nest-egg, he didn't think his mother would be searching his bedroom again. She had made no further mention of the incident, his rage, her remorse, her undertaking to replace the stolen money. She seemed slightly afraid of him these days, and he was conscious of something that had been happening more and more the bigger he became: his physical size tended to instil a degree of fear in others. He didn't like this.

In one way, though, his rage had been effective. His mother had pulled herself together and made a determined effort to obtain a job. She was now a packer in a nearby biscuit factory. Rod was genuinely sorry for her and deeply concerned; he recalled something else his grandmother had said to him about her: "Peggy's always been looking for something, but she's never known what it is. One thing's certain, she's no good at choosing her company, never was. I'm sorry to have to say this, Rodney, but that's how she got involved with your father. Bad choice. For both of them. You're lucky, you've got the good blood of our line in your veins."

Rod wondered about this. Good blood or bad blood, there seemed to be a lot of liquid fertilizer mixed in with the red and white corpuscles the science teacher said everyone had.

On the first weekday, the Monday of the May school holidays, he put his plans into operation. His mother had to leave at a quarter past seven in time to clock in at the biscuit factory, so he stayed in his room until she had gone. After some breakfast, he went to the bathroom and opened the cupboard above the basin. Some of his father's things were still here: a corroded safety razor; a small stack of used and rusting blades; two discolored toothbrushes which looked so germ-laden they would probably cause instant decay; a half-bald shaving brush; a stick of shaving soap reduced to a cracked stump after not having been used for over eighteen months; and a bottle of hair restorer. Thus, with a fine array of toilet requisites at his disposal, Rod gave himself the second shave of his career. Even though he used the razor blade showing the least corrosion, he nicked himself a number of times and drew blood. He was pleased about this. Helped give him an older look, he thought.

At a school pageant he had been the Old Man of the Forest, and Mildred Ross, in charge of makeup, had darkened his eyebrows and drawn lines at the corners of his eyes, then down from his nostrils and at each side of his mouth. His mother's makeup things littered the bathroom shelves and ledges, so he had no trouble in locating an eyebrow pencil. He used a light touch, realizing he could be in danger of drawing attention to what he had done if he used the pencil too heavily.

When it came to dressing, he put on one of his father's shirts—he was only just able to button it at the neck—and found a tie to go with it. Horrie's suit was loose around the middle, but alarmingly short in the legs and arms. And the hat was too small, but he wore it nevertheless, trying it first on the back of his head, but deciding it gave him an older and more responsible appearance by tilting it forward over his face. As for footwear, it was the same as at the school dance—brown socks and Horrie's reconditioned sandals.

He tried to give himself a strong manly profile as he set out at a swinging gait, and he was encouraged (after being at first panic-stricken) when he passed Mrs. Riordan. Thin and stooped, bent over as if from living in a low-roofed cave, making it necessary for her to wear smoke-tinted glasses when out in the sunlight, she gave him a quick friendly smile, something which would hardly have been forthcoming had she recognized him as the potential rapist she had claimed him to have been. But then her eyesight was very poor.

After walking all the way to the Town Hall, he picked up a blank enlistment form at the recruiting depot there, then continued along George Street and turned up Barrack Street to the State Lottery Office, where he had been taken by his grandmother when she had come into the city during one of her visits to Ultimo. "You've got to be in it to win it," she had told him as she filled in her form. Now Rod used lottery office pen and ink to fill in his enlistment form. He changed his surname from Murray to McKenzie, his mother's maiden name and his grandmother's married name, and gave his grandmother as his next-of-kin and her address as his own. He was quite sure she wouldn't mind him taking this liberty. He put back his date of birth to make himself twenty, the minimum for acceptance; but since he wasn't twenty-one he had to have the permission of a parent or guardian. So he decided that his grandmother would be his guardian and crossed George Street to the GPO to forge her signature, using the pen and ink provided in the telegrams section this time.

Now for the key move in the exercise. Out into Martin Place to join a line of what Horrie would call "cannon fodder" at the recruiting hut. He was pleased to note that in terms of physical size he was one of the biggest there, certainly the tallest. On the other hand, he was conscious that he probably looked the youngest, even though he kept squaring his chin and trying to fill out the chest of Horrie's suit.

Soon he found himself having to face a heavily-built sergeant wearing Great War campaign ribbons. He was told to take a seat in front of the desk as the sergeant relit his pipe. He studied Rod's enlistment form, then exhaled and eyed the recruit through a screen of pungent gray pipe smoke.

"If this is your date of birth, you're twenty. Is that correct?" the sergeant asked.

"Yes, sir," Rod replied, reaching down in his throat for the deepest vocal chords.

"Why do you want to enlist?"

Why? Rod wasn't prepared for what seemed to be such an unnecessary question, especially when posters everywhere exhorted men to join the colors, whether army, navy, or air force. He hadn't pondered on his motive. To vindicate himself in the eyes of a young lady? To head for the scene of the war on one of the great liners of the seven seas? He

— 57

wasn't ready to offer either explanation. Instead, he came up with an answer, even if it did sound like something Prickle-head Hillyard might have said: "To serve my country, sir."

"You won't do much serving if you end up in jail," the sergeant said, using the stem of his pipe to indicate where Rod had signed his name. "That your signature?"

"Yes, sir." Even though it was his "McKenzie" version.

"It says on this form that it's an offense to make a false attestation. Did you read that?"

"Yes, sir." Rod had read the warning, but had decided to ignore it.

"If you were to be accepted on the basis of this form, pass the medical examination, and then go to some theater of war and take part in an action which resulted in the death of an enemy soldier, do you realize what could happen?"

Maybe get a medal? But Rod didn't say this. He felt that his pose and disguise were fast failing him. He tried to shake his head, but found himself so stiff with apprehension that all he could manage was a twitch.

"You could be charged with 'Illegally Killing the King's Enemies.' We get too many would-be volunteers wasting our time. Not just youngsters like yourself, but men old enough to know better. Earlier this morning there was a bloke in here swearing he was only thirty-nine when I clearly remember seeing him last Anzac Day marching with the Boer War veterans." He tore the form in half and handed it back to Rod. "How old are you? Sixteen?"

Rod was so surprised at this assumption, and so elated by it, that he hastened to agree. "Yes, sir. That's right, sir. Sixteen."

"I guessed as much." And waving Rod out of the hut,

he added, "Don't come back here for another four years."

Four years be blowed, thought Rod as he emerged back exhilarated despite the rejection into Martin Place: if he thinks I'm sixteen now, it mightn't be all that long before someone takes me for a genuine twenty.

4

Rod became offsider to the yardman at the milk and ice depot. He regarded it as work which would enable him to look older by building up his muscles, so he revelled in the manual labor, shifting milk cans and crates of cream bottles, carrying blocks of ice in steel clamps, humping bales of hay for the horses, and burdening himself with masses of heavy leather and metal harnesses and trappings.

At the same time he began to shave more often to try to encourage the growth of the hair on his face. He applied some of the hair restorer to his cheeks and jowls in the hope that it might turn fuzz into bristles, even though it had a fierce sting, especially when he had nicked himself.

As far as working footwear was concerned, the depot solved Rod's problem by supplying him with calf-length gum boots for cleaning out stables and hosing down the yards. He also wore them when helping out Horrie at night.

On one such night, he took the elevator to the top of a block of apartments in Elizabeth Bay and spent a few minutes on the flat roof, looking down and around the starlit harbor, with the ships only partly outlined by their lights.

Carrying his can of milk, dipper, and small hand-crate of bottles of cream, Rod worked his way down the block and along the corridors floor by floor, his footsteps making no sound as the building was carpeted throughout. Each flat had a service cupboard with two small doors, one within the flat and bolted on that side, the second opening into the corridor. Here customers placed their receptacles, orders, and cash. On the fourth floor down, Rod quietly removed a crystal jug with a lace cover, weighted around the edges by colored beads. This was Jennifer Kinton's flat; she was an actress in radio and theater. Light showed in the chinks of the inner cupboard door and also under the main entrance door to the apartment. A note said two pints, which meant two full dippers and a bit from the can. He lifted off the jug cover as quietly as possible, but the beads tinkled on the crystal, and moments later the apartment door opened and Jennifer Kinton peered out, wearing a green négligée, her hair flaming red.

"Oh," she gasped. "Pardon me. I thought it was Horace."

"I'm helping him tonight," Rod explained.

"He's all right, then?"

"Yeah. He's working on some of the other blocks."

"Deserted me?" she said with exaggerated mock hurt.

"I dunno about that," Rod said, a stranger to such talk.

"Only teasing, darling. Perhaps you'd like to come in for a drink instead."

The invitation plunged Rod into such a quandary that he scratched his head for guidance, forgetting that the same hand was grasping the handle of his dipper, with the result that a spoonful of milk ran down the side of his face.

In an instant the actress had found a lace handkerchief tucked into the top of her négligée and used it to dab the milk off his cheek. Then she took his arm, drew him inside the apartment and closed the door. She was English and had settled in Australia after a stage tour in which she had played opposite her husband.

"Now what would you care for?" she asked him, indicating a trolley crammed with drinks and glasses.

"None of that stuff, thanks," said Rod quickly, assuming all the drinks were alcoholic.

"Something soft, then?"

"Thanks," said Rod, dazed by the luxurious surroundings into which he had been suddenly thrust, especially by the wall-to-ceiling windows with their panoramic harbor view.

As she opened a bottle of orange cordial and filled a crystal tumbler for him, he spotted something mounted on a tripod and pointing out the big window: a telescope. Handing him the drink, the actress said, "My husband claimed to be a keen ship-watcher, although I think he sometimes spent most of the time aiming at the girls sunbathing in the nude on the tops of flats."

She giggled naughtily as Rod gulped the orange drink. "Go ahead and have a look," she urged him. "Not at the rooftops—nothing there this hour, I'm afraid."

Even the bone socket of Rod's eye seemed to be tingling as he fitted it to the viewing end of the telescope, while his hostess leaned over him to show him how to control the focus. The effect was miraculous. What had been just a vague shape, tenuously held together by a nucleus of lights, became a freighter. It was as if the telescope had the power to penetrate darkness. But he could revel in the magic of this only in a limited way since the lady's closeness, and the touch of her breast on his shoulder through the silk, were disturbing and distracting, so he hastened to empty his glass, after which he looked for somewhere to place it, only to have her take it from his hand, saying, "Let me fill it again."

"Thanks all the same," he said, picking up the milk can and dipper, and the crate of cream—and to his dismay seeing that the damp bottom of the can had left a ring on the mauve carpet. "I'll have to get on with the round."

He made for the door and tried to open it with the hand holding the crate. She opened it for him, allowing him to escape, and when he muttered, "Thanks for the drink," she fluttered her fingertips, as Mildred Ross had done, but without the sports mistress's captivating touch.

He was glad to complete the deliveries on that floor, and glad when he had done the whole building. He had been afraid of becoming involved in what might be a betrayal of a certain self-imposed fidelity, should he have surrendered to what could have been the consequence of remaining much longer in that actress's apartment. He said nothing about the encounter to Horrie, but that didn't stop the milk carter from finding out. A week or so later, one cool, wet winter morning, about the time the news came through that the Germans had done the unbelievable and invaded Russia, Horrie returned shivering to the depot.

He shuddered and crisscrossed his arms and patted his shoulders to warm himself up, then gave Rod a light dig in the ribs. "You didn't do too bad for yourself last week."

"Whadda you mean?" Rod asked, steeling himself for more of Horrie's leg-pulling.

"Actress with her husband back in England with his regiment."

"Fair go!" Rod said. "All I did was have an orange drink—and a squizz through that telescope she's got there."

"All the same, she was impressed. Nice strapping young

man, she told me." Horrie tried to prod Rod's ribs again, only to find two fists clenched and raised. So Horrie laughed and said, "You could do all right for yourself there."

But Rod didn't entertain any such thought. He couldn't. His loyalty lay elsewhere. Over the previous weekend he had seen Brenda King walking side by side with a college boy in a school cadet uniform. While this caused him a jealous pang, it also made him more determined.

Rod had returned Horrie's sandals, suit, and hat, but this didn't mean he had given up plans to try to enlist again. Far from it. Now that he was earning a weekly wage of fifteen shillings he calculated that it wouldn't take too long before he could afford a suit and hat of his own, and a new pair of boots. That is, if he protected his savings against the danger of further theft, which he did by placing the money in an empty screw-top jam jar and burying it beside the lean-to shed at the back of the cottage.

By the end of his fourth week at the depot, he felt he could afford a trip to Parramatta to see his grandmother. From the station there a bus ran every hour to where she lived, but as usual he walked the distance.

As always, she was delighted to see him and what she told him couldn't have pleased him more, even though it repeated something apparently said by Miss Jennifer Kinton. "My word, Rodney, you really are growing up into a fine strapping young man."

The locality was well above sea level and the air noted for its purity. She lived here because it was kinder to her asthma. Even so, Rod had to endure seeing her stop in the middle of a sentence and have to fight for her breath. At such times she would seem even smaller, somehow like a punctured football bladder, trying to inflate herself again.

She always managed to do so, and would carry on talking where she had been forced to leave off, as if nothing had intervened.

In the company of the one person in the world he felt he could trust, Rod told his grandmother about his first attempt to enlist and that he was planning a second; that he would be changing his surname to McKenzie, putting her down as his next-of-kin and using her address as his own.

"That's fine by me, Rodney," she said. "I'm sure you know what you're doing. Your ancestors were level-headed men, and you've inherited that. Peggy got nothing of it, as far as I can see. Skipped a generation and missed her out, the way it sometimes does. How is she, anyway?"

Rod was able to give a reasonably favorable report. His mother had held her job at the biscuit factory, even though she had missed two Mondays due to too much imbibing over the weekend. No, there was still no word from his father. He had been in the Middle East early enough to have been in either the Desert or Greek campaigns.

Rod never visited without mowing the patch of grass at the front and clipping the hedges, then going shopping with the old lady. It was out shopping on one occasion that she had met a fragile friend struggling with baskets of groceries and greens and said, "My grandson, Rodney, will be very happy to help you, I'm sure." That was how his services to the aged and frail had begun and had continued, until he had fallen foul of Mrs. Riordan.

Back at Ultimo, Rod discovered that his mother was capable on occasion of putting two and two together, despite his grandmother's views to the contrary. So he had been to see Grandma? Where did he get the money? Rod said that he worked every Friday night with Horrie Benson, and a second night every other week. Unfortunately, someone had mentioned to his mother that her son didn't appear to be going to school any longer. And so it came out that for a month he had been in the employ of the milk and ice company.

Since his performance after discovering the loss of his nest-egg, she had been wary of upsetting him. Now she was so angry that her caution deserted her. Besides, she had been drinking, and at such times was aggressive. It was something he accepted, especially after what his grandmother had told him: "They say that when the wine's in, the mind's out. With Peggy, it's like someone else's mind. That of a complete stranger."

"So you've been cheating me all this time!" she cried.

"*Cheating* you?"

"Working all these weeks, earning money, and not even paying me a penny for board and lodging!"

The need to pay, any obligation to pay, had not entered into his head. After what she had taken from that tobacco tin, she was still in his debt, even if it was one she chose to forget.

"You could have landed me in jail, too. As soon as you start work, the army allowance for you stops. Five shillings a week. You didn't think about that, did you?"

No, he had to admit, he hadn't.

"You're not staying under this roof unless you pay," she said. "How much are you getting a week?"

So he told her, and she shocked him by promptly demanding exactly half.

"Seven and six?" he protested.

"Try and get board and lodging for that anywhere else!"

Rod didn't know enough about this to argue. He had thought of moving out to live with his grandmother, but the return train fares would limit his savings. And he had to stay locally if he was going to work at nights with Horrie. Besides, living so far away meant he would have to forego the occasional glimpse of Brenda King. It seemed he had no alternative but to agree.

"If you've been working four weeks already that means you owe me thirty shillings."

Now he really did protest. "But you stole my boots money!"

Confronted with this, she chose not to argue; but she had a different issue to take up.

"I believe you've been at the beck and call of the Kings again."

"I've done a few odd jobs," he admitted.

"You know how I feel about that stuck-up Helen King, so don't do it. If you want any odd jobs, there are plenty around here."

Rod couldn't agree more. From the front gate to the back fence, the whole place was a collection of odd jobs crying out for attention, but whatever he might do he would only find himself criticized, so he decided to be guided by another of his grandmother's sayings: "A blind eye's a very handy thing to have in this life, Rodney—never be afraid to use it."

A few weeks later, at Elizabeth Bay, Rod was just about finishing another night's round with Horrie, doing his last block of apartments, when a mighty voice spoke from the middle of the harbor. The *Queen Mary* sounded her siren, a deep reverberating blast that echoed around the length and breadth of the harbor, into every bay and inlet, every crevice in the rocks, starting the lions roaring in reply at Taronga Park Zoo.

He raced to the top of the block and saw that the great

liner had actually weighed anchor. With tugs clustering around her and some six thousand troops on board this trip, she was leaving to take her place in another convoy for the secret destination which everyone now knew would be Suez via Fremantle and Ceylon. What an occasion to view her departure through a powerful telescope!

Thus it was that he succumbed to the temptation of dragging the cover off Miss Jennifer Kinton's jug so that the beads striking the crystal turned the receptacle into a musical instrument. Its tune had the desired effect; soon after Rod had filled the jug, the door of the apartment opened.

"Oh, it's you!" she said, her eyes eager. The hoped-for invitation was prompt in coming. "Care for an orange cordial? Or have you moved on to something a little more adventurous?"

"That'll be fine," he said. "Orange cordial."

"Then why don't you come in?"

He realized he had been standing flat-footed with the milk can and dipper in one hand, the crate of cream in the other.

As she closed the door after him, he was lured to the wall window, now framing the *Queen Mary* being escorted and guided down the harbor by her brood of tugs, smoke streaming into the dark sky from her three funnels. He glanced at the telescope and Jennifer Kinton read his thoughts.

"Go ahead."

He stooped down, fitted his eye to the viewing piece, aimed it and adjusted the focus. There had been no send-off to the ship, but troops were crowded on her decks. He recalled that on a recent Sunday afternoon visit to the Domain, a speaker had claimed that the two *Queens* and other transports were nothing more than giant hearses, and that a white cross should be painted on each ship's side for every man who had been killed after having been a passenger.

His hostess touched his shoulder and he took the glass of orange cordial. Then a big swig.

"No need to rush, you know," she said with a coo which unfortunately reminded him of Prickle-head Hillyard's voice when the teacher had turned amorous. "It must be a long night for you."

"Not really," said Rod, who always found the round passed quickly.

She took his free hand and he knotted up throughout, but put up no resistance as she led him away from the telescope on its tripod. "Let's go inside. The bedroom's dark and that makes the view so much better."

It didn't occur to Rod to question why the lounge lights could not have been turned out instead. She sat him beside her on the edge of a large double bed, saying, "Now, isn't that a better view?"

"Probably is," he said, gulping his drink.

"Your feet must get terribly tired running up and down all the stairs—especially in those huge boots. Why don't you take them off?"

The gum boots were the biggest size available and his feet hadn't quite caught up with them yet, so they remained comfortable despite all the stairs. He remembered that his socks had potato-sized holes in them. Before he could make up his mind one way or the other, his hostess had hauled the boots off his feet, releasing a sweaty stink. But the actress did not appear to be offended by the odor. She took the empty glass from him and placed it on a small occasional table. She had something else to offer him now. She took his cheeks between her flared hands, the front of her négligée falling open as she pressed her mouth to his, and as the *Queen Mary* passed through the defensive submarine boom between Chowder Bay on the north side and Shark Point opposite, he began to surrender to being taken across one of the divides between youth and manhood. A pity he wasn't fronting up to a recruiting sergeant in the morning, he thought: he might have a pair of adult-looking bags under his eyes, like Horrie's, to show for the experience.

As her mouth spread and moved over his lips, he kept his eyes open just enough to be able to follow the final passage of the *Queen Mary* through Sydney Heads and out into the open ocean; and just enough for him to discern, farther out, an incoming shape similar to that of the departing transport. Almost identical in fact.

With roving caresses, Jennifer Kinton had started to ease him down onto the soft quilted eiderdown; but he found himself resisting as he realized that he was about to be a witness, as long as he didn't give himself over completely to the pleasures being lavished on him, to one of the ultimate moments in the annals of maritime magic, the *Queen Mary* going out through Sydney Heads and passing her younger but slightly larger sister ship on her way in to pick up another quota of troops. There could be no doubt the incoming giant was the *Queen Elizabeth*, because her two funnels, in contrast to the three of the other ship, were distinguishable in the gray light breaking along the eastern horizon.

So that he could partake of the passing of the two leviathans at closer quarters, he broke free of the increasingly ardent embrace of his hostess and ran through into the adjoining lounge to use the telescope on the tripod. Thus he caught the actual moment of passing. As a seafaring spectacle there could be nothing more sublime, except seeing the two *Queens* anchored at the same time in the most beautiful harbor in the world; and that, because of the hazard to both vessels, could never happen.

Undoubtedly, he would have stayed crouched at the telescope to watch the *Queen Elizabeth* pass in through the boom then weave her way up the harbor on the sinuous track left by her older sister on the surface of the water, but kith and kin of an altogether different kind put an end to that. One of his gum boots hit him on the shoulder, the other on his rump, both thrown from the bedroom doorway to the accompaniment of an outburst worthy of the Domain on a lively Sunday afternoon, about the manly shortcomings of local milk vendors.

———————

And so it was that without bags under his eyes, but in new suit, hat, and size thirteen boots, Rod set out for the second time to try to enlist, sucking an old pipe of his grandfather's picked up during his last visit to his grandmother. It was minus tobacco, but he thought it might help to give him an older look. Again, he had successfully nicked himself when shaving.

As he had worked all through the previous day, the yardman gave him Monday free. He walked to the Town Hall once more, savoring his stout new boots, which were black to match his navy suit. After picking up an enlistment form, he headed in a different direction this time, up to Hyde Park, along its paths past the Anzac War Memorial, then into Oxford Street, which he followed all the way to Victoria Barracks in Paddington. He made two stops, one at a post office to fill in most of the form, the other at a Commonwealth Savings Bank, where he used a different pen and ink to forge his grandmother's signature again. Maggie McKenzie, as his guardian giving him permission to volunteer. He still had a week to go until his fifteenth birthday.

At the Barracks, the enlistment line was shorter and the atmosphere upexpectedly relaxed and friendly, the reason being that there had been a very heavy night in all the messes after a rugby league football match, officers and warrant officers versus the rest. Enlistment papers were passed with a minimum of scrutiny, volunteers being asked to do little more than confirm that the main signatures on the forms were their own before being passed through for medical examination at a building in the showgrounds behind the Barracks. If this proved to be another formality, then in no time Rod would have his hand on a copy of the Holy Bible, affirming his allegiance to King and country.

Alas, at the medical center life was being taken very seriously. There had been no celebrations among the medical officers and therefore no hangovers. Each volunteer was subjected to stringent examinations by teams of two doctors—and the pair in whose hands Rod found himself were both Great War veterans, one as rigorous as the other. After their individual examinations of Rod, they put their heads together and conferred in low tones.

Running a gritty hand over Rod's cheeks and chin, the elder of the two said, "Not much chance of swinging on your whiskers yet." Then he plucked at his pubic hair. "And not much here to show for yourself, either. Sorry, son." And the other doctor began to nod. "It's our agreed opinion you're only sixteen."

Sixteen! Rod revealed nothing of his disappointment, but felt he had made no progress in his campaign to look older since his first attempt. That may only have been two months ago, but in a way it was an age—in that time the *Queen Mary* and the *Queen Elizabeth* made round trips from Sydney to Suez and back.

5

Rod was not despondent for long. After all, he could take some comfort in the fact that even though he was technically still only fourteen, he had been judged by a shrewd doctor to be sixteen. So, as he turned fifteen a week later, he set about planning his next attempt to obtain one of those hats which appeared on one of the recruiting posters; slouch hats turned up at the side with a metal rising sun badge and the caption: "Soldier, Here's Your Hat."

He had a growing awareness of what was behind such posters. He had seen the *Queen Mary* unloading the casualties brought back from the Middle East, the ambulances lined up at the wharves at Woolloomooloo as tenders ferried the maimed, the merely wounded, and the sick ashore. Among the ratbags in the Domain there were some earnest and honest speakers who tried to make it clear that freedom was at stake in this war. Rod believed them; there was now more to his quest for a uniform than the desire to impress a fair member of the opposite sex.

The medical officer at the showgrounds had given Rod something to think about when he had commented on his lack of beard and paucity of pubic hair. There were at least two ways of trying to remedy this deficiency. First of all, experiment with some of his father's hair restorer, which had been intended for a pate rapidly becoming prematurely denuded. By applying it around the region of his private parts it might encourage some of the luxuriant growth the label on the bottle promised. On the other hand he might try to augment what was already there by adding false hair stuck on with gum arabic, as actors did when wearing false beards.

A member of the local community regularly applied false hair to his face—Mr. Yarls Finnigan, who claimed mixed Scandinavian and Irish descent, and an early career of promise on the London stage. He was known as the Duke-and-Duchess. For a week or two he would be seen walking out with a cane, and sporting a beard or old-fashioned side levers, the soul of courtesy to all he encountered, bowing, wishing them the best of health. It was rumored that he had private means in the form of an allowance regularly paid into his bank by a family who wished him to live as far away from them as possible. He had a flat in one of the former mansions in the locality. At other times, again for a week or two, he would be clean-shaven and highly made-up for his role as the Duchess, wearing long frocks, high-heeled shoes, hats adorned with flowers and long gloves, and his voice, which in his role as the Duke was mellow and deep, would be high and falsetto.

Mrs. Riordan and her Christian cronies considered that he should be put away, but most accepted him as a harmless eccentric who interfered with no one. Rod wondered if Mr. Finnigan could help him to sport a temporary moustache at least.

While he was contemplating such moves, one of his

— 74

mother's weekend binges resulted in her being incapable of going to work on either the following Monday or Tuesday, so she was fired by the biscuit factory. The half of his wages which he handed over to her was her only money until her allowances arrived, something which she admitted tearfully as she tried to thank him and promised to mend her ways. He felt for her, as if she, too, had an affliction, an inborn incapacity, far worse than the clumsiness which continued to plague him and land him in trouble.

As had happened on the electric train to Parramatta. Groping his way between the seats to be near the door once the train stopped, he trod heavily on a projecting foot, that of a military policeman who brayed with pain and threatened, "Bloody lucky you're not in an army uniform or I'd have you!"

"Sorry," Rod said, hastening to add, "it was an accident."

"Oh, yeah?" said the military policeman, much more inclined to believe it was a deliberate act.

The train pulled up so sharply that Rod had to grab the edge of a seat. He was conscious of the hostile glare that followed him out of the train, and through the carriage window as he moved along in the line to hand in his ticket to the collector; but on reflection he was heartened by the encounter. The military policeman had seemed to assume that he was old enough to be in uniform. And so his boots seemed to sing all the long walk to his grandmother's place.

Regarding his mother's dismissal from the biscuit factory, Rod was able to report that she had managed to secure another job. At one of the new munitions factories as a packer.

"She's good enough at things when she tries, so we can only hope," his grandmother said. While Rod regarded the old lady as a font of native wisdom, she herself claimed there were things to which she had no answer. "I wish the Good Lord had given me a few more brains," she had told him. It had surprised him that a line of big men could throw up such a tiny female. That is, until she said to him, "I was born a bit of a sprite to preserve the line. That's nature's way. Suddenly there's a little 'un to make sure the blood stays strong for the big 'uns that come along after. Like you, Rodney."

He didn't tell her that he had failed in his second attempt to enlist. Just that he hoped it wouldn't be too long before he was wearing one of those hats in the recruiting poster.

Whether it was the effect of the hair restorer or just normal growth (if growth in Rod's case could ever have been regarded as normal), he was sure that his pubic hair had become thicker. His beard was certainly sprouting faster, and he needed to shave more than once a week now. If he left his upper lip untouched, the beginnings of a dark moustache were visible, however sparse.

His yardman had joined the air force as a groundsman, so Rod was now in charge, doing the work of his boss as well as his own. But the depot manager hadn't awarded him a raise, claiming that he couldn't do so because of Rod's age. Well, he wasn't going to worry about that. According to his plan, he wouldn't be at the depot all that much longer. Because of the two rejections he had received, just getting into the army had become an objective in itself, apart from any motive he might have for wanting to wear the uniform.

On an October weekend when the Germans were attacking Moscow, and the Allied Army in the Western Desert was preparing to launch an offensive, Rod again sighted Brenda with the college boy wearing his school cadet uniform and slouch hat. Some days later, on his way home from the depot one evening, he met Fran. She was breathless to tell him the news that someone else they knew would soon be in uniform—Mildred Ross. She had been invited to join the AWAS, the newly formed Australian Women's Army Service, as a physical instructress, and to train to become an officer.

"How's your furniture?" Rod asked her.

Fran gave an easy laugh. "Mum hasn't started talking about moving it again, so you're safe for the moment."

He grinned, but then Fran frowned, and his face clouded.

"Brenda's been going out with an awful drip," she said. "His mother helps at the officers' club, like Mum—that's how they met. He's in his school cadets."

"I've seen him," said Rod.

"He's never out of that uniform. I think he sleeps in it. Must be nuts."

Rod was naturally delighted to hear this and to sense something of why Fran spoke in this vein. She regarded Rod's devotion to Brenda as most romantic. No boy had ever carried *her* schoolbag home, let alone regularly. She wasn't at all jealous. Anything but. She wanted the relationship between Rod and Brenda to flourish, despite the strictures her mother's influence had put on her sister's conduct.

Changing the subject, and surprising Rod, Fran said, "It must be wonderful working at that depot."

He enjoyed the work, but he had no reason to enthuse about it. "All those horses," she said, and then he began to understand. "I love horses. And I wish we still lived back near your place."

"Why's that?" he squawked. This he could not comprehend.

"To be near that horse-trough. It must be like having horses as visitors."

"Their visiting cards are very good for the garden, too," he said, grinning, repeating what his grandmother had said about a pile of horse manure she had seen near the trough on one of her visits to Ultimo.

They parted, Fran giving him a very sweet smile, one which he could not help but transfer to the lips of his image of her elder sister.

It was now that he seriously considered seeking some help from the Duke-and-Duchess before mounting his third attempt to enlist as a real soldier. It was going to be a long time before the shadow on his upper lip developed into a moustache, so perhaps he could obtain a false one for the day. He had never actually spoken to Mr. Yarls Finnigan in either of his roles, although as Duke his cane had been raised to Rod in a brief greeting and as Duchess he had bestowed a gushing red smile. Mr. Finnigan was the star guest at the converted mansion, occupying part of the ground floor at the rear, facing a grassy patch. His door was reached by a side path, as Rod knew because he had been there once to deliver milk when the carter on the round fell ill and Horrie had deputized, doing a double shift with Rod's help. The Duke-and-Duchess had left an unusual receptacle on his doorstep with a note written with a flourish, requesting one pint—a pewter mug with an enameled coat of arms on it, one that suggested it might be an important family crest.

While Rod was basically a shy person, unsure of himself because he lived with unpredictability, never knowing when he was suddenly going to be the victim of his own ineptitude again, deep down he was of a determined nature. Once he had set himself to do anything, it became an issue, even if only within himself; and while he never conveyed anything about such internal conflicts to anyone, if he failed to measure up to his self-set standards he considered himself to have failed. Thus he found himself with no alternative but to at least call on Yarls Finnigan—especially as he had a strong feeling that a moustache could do the trick for him. He had experimented. First of all by using one of his mother's eyebrow pencils to draw a Clark Gable style of moustache on his upper lip. Then, after smearing that same area with soap, he had stuck on strands of black horsehair from a split in the seat of one of the ancient leather armchairs in the sitting room.

On a hot morning in early December, a Monday, his free day from the depot to make up for being on duty over the weekend, he felt the time had come to make this call. It was a day so glorious that it seemed utter desecration that somewhere some inhabitants of the planet would be squinting along the barrels of rifles, traversing huge naval guns, releasing bombs from high-flying aircraft, intent on annihilating one another.

The door to Mr. Finnigan's flat was open and led immediately into his sitting room, where he now sat in a lightweight dressing gown, wearing neither false hair nor heavy makeup, neither the Duke nor the Duchess, just a rather small man in his mid-thirties, obviously in distress. Tears had dampened his cheeks and he reacted to Rod's arrival as if it was timely that a Good Samaritan should come to him at this moment. He had an opened letter in his hand and held it out for Rod to read. Rod had to step inside the flat to take it, a routine printed letter, an army call-up notice instructing Yarls Finnigan, of this address in Ultimo, to report the next day at Victoria Barracks, Paddington, and to bring two cut lunches with him.

As Rod looked up from reading the notice, the recipient said, "I don't know what to do, dear boy. I don't think I could ever cope with the company of the common herd . . . especially all those men."

To Rod, this presented an opportunity, and he seized on it. "How about if I go in your place?"

"Oh, but they'll be after you, too. Every man and boy. Don't you know—the Japanese Empire has entered the war. Pearl Harbor has been bombed and destroyed. We're all in it now."

This came as no surprise to Rod. For months it had been rumored that Japan would be joining forces with the German-Italian Axis. He had seen the signs during his rounds of the apartment blocks. Woolbuyers and other members of the Japanese community had closed or sold their flats. Four months ago the last Japanese passenger and freight ship had headed home, having maintained a regular monthly link by way of Manila and Hong Kong with such Japanese seaports as Kobe, Osaka, Yokohama, and Nagasaki.

By Christmas, without any help from a false moustache, he was in uniform. Private Rodney McKenzie. He had enlisted at Parramatta. It had been simple and straightforward. No one had questioned his age, the strength of his beard, the dearth or otherwise of pubic hair, such was the national panic to increase the numbers of the armed forces now that war was so much closer to home shores.

He was posted to an infantry training unit based at Ingleburn camp, and here issued with attire and equipment. There was only one size .303 rifle, one size bayonet and scabbard, the same going for mess tins, enamel mug, ground sheet, and other items; but when it came to clothing, Private McKenzie posed problems. At the quartermaster's store, they managed to find a felt hat large enough, trousers, tunic, socks, drawers, singlets; in fact everything except boots. The largest size issued was thirteen, the same as the black boots he had bought, but these were already pinching his feet. And the brown issue boots of this size, which hadn't yet been broken in, were tight to the extent of being too small. So the QM sergeant had to measure his feet and requisition specially made boots. In the meantime, he had written permission to wear the black ones.

He was required to make a will. A will? For small collections of cigarette cards, stamps, marbles, his miniature motorcars, a few model ships including his *Queen Mary*? It was pointed out to him that he would be receiving pay and he might well build up a handsome cash credit, so he would need to leave it to someone. He thought he ought to remember his mother, but he had claimed she was dead, so he wrote: "I hereby bequeath my whole estate to my grandmother Maggie McKenzie." One of the two witnesses to his signature was the advising officer.

Despite all this, the truth was he was underage, very much so. He had to be on his guard—and he was aware of the danger to which he was exposing himself just by being in the Ultimo area, even though protected by the false surname under which he had enlisted.

Returning home in uniform for the first time, he found his mother drinking with a new woman friend from the munitions factory; but her presence didn't curb his mother's tongue.

"I've been worried stiff about you," she began, revealing genuine concern. But the wine was in again, and the mind was out, even if, as his grandmother had said, it was that of a stranger. "Where the hell have you been, anyway? And where's your board and lodgings money?"

And then, but only then, possibly because it had become a daily sight to see every other male in uniform, did she realize that he was in khaki.

"I'm in the army," he told her.

"I can see that," she said, and the grasping stranger spoke through her again. "How much are you getting paid?"

"Five shillings a day."

"I'll expect some of that."

Stung into protesting, he cried, "What for? I won't be here. I won't be needing any board and lodgings."

Stumped by his logical response, she still had ideas about what he should do with his money. "I'll look after it for you. Put it aside for you. Build up a nice nest-egg for you."

Her new-found friend, eyes moist with booze and sentiment, said, "What a lovely idea for him, Peggy."

Like fun, Rod thought. Remembering the fate of an earlier nest-egg, he made no reply, but left his mother and her friend to continue to dispose of the contents of a bottle of cheap Muscat, and set out to call on Horrie Benson, who would be getting out of bed about this time in the afternoon.

Horrie was up, but still half-asleep. His wife and kids thought Rod looked mighty in his uniform. Presently they were left alone together, and Horrie, keeping his voice low, said, "I'm whacked. That Miss Jennifer Kinton! Struth! You don't know what you passed up."

Rod had no regrets; he didn't need those bags under his eyes now. He was in. Horrie had trusted him, so Rod believed he could speak in confidence.

"I don't have to tell you, do I, that I got in underage."

"Listen, sport," Horrie said. "You don't have to tell me any bloody thing if you don't want to."

But Rod did. He revealed that he had enlisted under his grandmother's name. He would like to write to Horrie, and hear back. But that would mean putting his army name, number, and unit on his letter, something which might be seen by Horrie's wife or kids.

"No problem," Horrie said. "Write to me care of the depot. Wouldn't be the first time I've received letters there." He winked. "Joe, the manager, doesn't ask any questions."

So that was settled, and after having jokingly told Horrie to give his regards to Edgar, he moved on to pay another local visit.

Before turning the corner which would take him past the fronts of the row of cottages in which the Kings lived, Rod heard some hammering. It was Fran, out on the footpath, trying to nail back a loose paling on the picket fence. He crept silently toward her, and for once seemed in no danger of losing his balance, thanks to the long hours of parade-ground drill and route marches, all of which seemed to have coordinated his working parts—his arms and hands, legs and feet, head and eyes—so that instead of operating independently of one another, often with disastrous results, they now did so in unison. On the rifle range, after failing to hit the targets for a start, he had settled down and was showing outstanding promise as a marksman.

"Need a hand?" he asked.

Fran gasped, not recognizing him at first. "Rod!" she cried. And as he took the hammer from her, she said, "Since when have you been in the . . . ?" She was going to say the school cadets, but stopped herself, realizing that he couldn't possibly be one of them as he didn't go to the right sort of school. Besides, she saw that he was wearing the uniform of a fully-fledged soldier.

Hearing their voices, Brenda appeared through the open front door, standing on the tiled patio. Her immediate question was the dangerous sort that Rod feared.

"How did you get in?" she asked him.

"The way things are," he said with forced bravado, "they're accepting anyone."

Which was largely true. In the month that had passed since he had been sworn in, the Japanese had swarmed south as far as the Netherlands East Indies. As he used the claw of the hammer to extract bent nails from the paling, then straightened them on the concrete edge of the footpath, he told the two sisters that he would soon be going to a jungle warfare school.

Using the salvaged nails, he secured the loose paling again. Another odd job done, he returned the hammer to Fran, who gave him a look of gratitude which was admiring at the very least, and could well have been considered adoring, something which did not pass unnoticed by Brenda. She said: "You'll write to me, I hope."

Rod was unprepared for this, flattered, unaware that she had been mimicking her mother. When officers checked out after a stay at the club, Helen King often used these words. And she received some letters, all of which she replied to, regarding it as part of her war effort.

After recovering from the surprise of the invitation, Rod responded to it with an awkward, "If you'd like me to . . ."

But it would be most unlikely. A risk he couldn't take, not when he had to put his assumed surname on any letter he might write.

He looked back to Fran, concerned that he had snubbed her, although helpless to have done otherwise, still enslaved by certain indelible soft kisses.

Brenda noted his concern and was quick to take care of it. "I'll let Fran know what you say," she said.

Fran gave Rod a light shrug, a mannerism that she might have caught from him.

With his grandmother it was different. She already had his rank and surname. To these he added his army number and unit when he visited her outside Parramatta. He was a credit to his military ancestors, she told him, reaching up to claw hold of the sleeve of his tunic above the elbow and pull him down so that she could plant a dry kiss on his cheek. "Now you're in it, Rodney," she said, "the war's as good as won."

About this time there was a tragedy at Ultimo, reported in the newspapers. The Duke-and-Duchess finally put an end to his dual masquerade. The prospect of being cooped up with rough male company was more than he could face, so he placed his neck on an electric train line under a culvert not far from Central Railway Station.

Shortly after this, Rod's made-to-measure boots were delivered, two pairs of them with leather laces: he was ready to go north for training. He would be making his first sea voyage to the tropical island of New Guinea, but on a ship a mere tenth of the size of the *Queen Mary* or the *Queen Elizabeth*, which were being withdrawn from the run from Australia and across the Indian Ocean. It was not the disappointment which might have been expected, since something of his single-mindedness of purpose, his sense of dedication, which had been involved in his craze for the big ships, was becoming concentrated in another direction. He had begun to find himself committed to a cause.

Part
Two

6

Rod and other members of his platoon made a dash from the open doorway of one of the gray U.S. DC-3 transports, heading for weapon-pits, bunkers, and other unmanned emplacements on the edge of the Wau airstrip, each man his own packhorse.

Before landing, from the round perspex windows of the plane, all ribs and thin alloy skin, so spare that it might have passed through the hands of an aircraft taxidermist, they had glimpsed Japanese troops on surrounding spurs where the kunai grass merged with jungle. Beyond these spurs lay a dense-green sea of rising serrations of ridges and razorbacks and Stygian ravines. The airstrip slanted slightly uphill and was sodden from the drenching rains which had detained the incoming Australian troops in Port Moresby for four days.

Now jets of muddy water spurted where enemy bullets struck as the leader of Rod's section and two others made for a bunker, while Rod veered toward an open weapon-pit, the three normally on his heels following—Nugget Bates, Fred Mullen, and Larry Donald, all sharing with him the exalted rank of private. Like the other defensive positions, it had been built by the Wau garrison of local volunteers before they went forward into the mountains to try to at least delay the arrival of the Japanese force.

Diving one after the other into the pit, despite their cumbersome gear, they found themselves in murky water up to their thighs. Machine-gun fire from a spur was directed at them. Nugget, Mullen, and Donald let loose bursts from their submachine guns without locating the source of the enemy fire, but Rod, the only one to carry an issue .303 rifle, aimed to where the muzzle of a machine gun spat gouts of flame, the tall kunai grass mown down in front of it and forming a fire-lane. Behind the machine gun there was a peaked cloth cap just visible. Rod took careful aim, put the first pressure on his trigger, waited until after another flurry of enemy fire, then his rifle kicked as its firing-pin struck the cap of the bullet in his breach. From where the machine-gun flashes had come, an arm was flung up, and there was no further firing. It was for such marksmanship that Rod had been graded a first-class shot.

Smoke began to rise from Japanese positions after mortar bombs were lobbed on them. The air crackled and whined with rifle and submachine-gun fire. The transport planes kept lumbering in, disgorging stores, ammunition, weapons, including parts of lightweight twenty-five pounder guns, and troops. Some soldiers, after leaping nimbly from the planes, had to be dragged back on board, limp or writhing, dead or maimed just over an hour after setting out across the ranges from Port Moresby.

Mullen and Donald were veterans from the Middle East, brought back to Australia for jungle warfare training on the Atherton Tablelands in North Queensland. Rod and Nugget had also trained there and had joined the battalion as reinforcements. All had fought together in Papua and into New Guinea, through the putrid rain forest on the trail to Kokoda, and in the coconut and coffee plantations of Gona and Buna, little known outposts until they began to appear in headlines as major battlegrounds in war correspondents' dispatches.

The order was to occupy a position and settle in, so Rod and his mate Nugget, who was not much more than half Rod's size, manned the rim of the weapon-pit, one with an Owen submachine gun, the other with his rifle, while Donald and Mullen set about trying to improve conditions for all four by bailing out the water, then the mud.

Between the black-haired Nugget and Rod there was a mutual protectiveness. Rod tended to shepherd Nugget because he was so small; to Nugget, the other's very size seemed to make him somehow vulnerable and in need of safeguarding. As for the close association of Fred Mullen and Larry Donald, it was based neither on size, age, nor appearance. Mullen was old enough to be Donald's father; he was lean, with mahogany skin, slits for eyes, and it was rumored that when he was idling between the two big wars he had been convicted for coining, faking crude copies of florins. Donald was fresh-faced, with slightly bulbous blue eyes, and such a striking air of innocence that he tended to make himself suspect. He boasted that he had belonged to a gang of car thieves based in the western suburbs of Sydney; his job had been to take the stolen vehicles to bush hideouts, where they were painted different colors, their mileage meters wound back, and attempts made to alter engine numbers. The mateship of these two seemed to be based on mutual craftiness and opportunism.

As bailers, the pair were slapdash, until they reached mud and pebbles; and then it was that suddenly Donald thought he glimpsed twinkles in the muck. Peering closer, he saw more such twinkles, and although he had never done any prospecting, he was ready to believe that they were specks of precious metal. And so from bailing with an enamel mug he switched to panning with his mess tin, using water still seeping into the pit to dilute the mud.

"What the hell's goin' on?" Mullen wanted to know.

"I think I've struck gold," Donald announced.

This diverted the attention of both Rod and Nugget Bates, and Donald tilted the mess tin toward them so that they could see the few bright specks in the corner.

"So what?" said Mullen. "This is the Bulolo Valley, one of the richest strikes in the world. Alluvial gold. I remember blokes headin' here in droves when the rush was on."

Donald shook out some of the water and more glinting specks showed. "Look at this! The whole place must be lousy with the stuff."

"Arr," Mullen disparaged. "You'll have to scratch an' pan for a month of Sundays to get enough to fill your belly-button."

Despite his scepticism, however, Mullen detached his mess tin from the weighty load of gear which gave frontline soldiers, even though they carried only tropical kit, the appearance of overdressed hoboes. He started panning, too.

The urge was catching. Nugget was about to do the same, leaving Rod to look after the war on his own. Something which Rod didn't intend to do.

"Fair go!" he said.

And that was all he needed to say. Although the others knew he was younger than them and sometimes called him the Kid—and suspected that he was underage—he had a certain natural authority, something bound up with his size, yet at the same time a quality independent of it.

Having been reminded that they were not only in the thick of an ugly war again but also in a vulnerable position, Nugget and Fred Mullen stood to with their Owen guns; but Donald, reluctant to bow to any authority, especially coming from an overgrown kid, doggedly kept on panning— although he discovered that it took a myriad of specks to make anything of substance. He eventually gave up when word was passed from weapon-pits to bunkers to other emplacements that the Japanese were preparing to attack the airfield, but pulverizing artillery barrages from the swiftly-assembled twenty-five pounders forced the enemy into relinquishing their foxholes and bunkers.

Another twenty-four hours and the weapon-pit had dried out, except for some seepage. The four still manned it— and the supply planes still came in, at the rate of about sixty a day. From those in the next weapon-pit they had gathered that the Japanese were withdrawing along creek beds and jungle trails to mountain strongholds. This was confirmed when their platoon commander arrived with another officer. The former, Lieutenant Paine, had been a bank clerk, a pale, serious man of twenty-five.

The second officer, another lieutenant, boasted a distinctive bristling reddish moustache; he was introduced as an intelligence officer from battalion headquarters.

Despite the moustache, even before his name was mentioned, Rod had recognized the dreaded school scourge, Prickle-head Hillyard. He recalled that when last in Ultimo, Horrie Benson had passed on something picked up from his boy Spider; a hush-hush army school to which the schoolmaster had gone involved a high-pressure course in the Japanese language.

Rod kept the forward brim of his slouch hat angled down

over his face as the platoon commander said that Lieutenant Hillyard was anxious to have reports on anything unusual that might have been observed in enemy activities or tactics—not necessarily here and now, but later, should anyone come by such information. Also documents, notes, diaries, and the like.

Without being invited to do so, Hillyard took over. "I'm particularly anxious to avoid any delay in handing over such material. In this regard, I should warn you that there are severe penalties for anyone treating such items as souvenirs." And then, in his sharpest schoolmasterish manner, he aimed a rebuke, framed as a question, at much the largest of the four soldiers, one who, it would seem, had not been paying proper attention. "Is that clear, soldier?"

Paine gave Hillyard an angry look, openly resenting the other's liberty in calling one of his men to order. At the same time, as if slowly lifting a curtain, Rod raised the forward brim of his slouch hat and his eyes met Hillyard's with a steady stare, throwing the intelligence officer's eyes into a visible panic, their arrogant glare swiftly diminishing.

Rod was all too conscious of what he stood to lose should the man looming there above the weapon-pit point the finger at him for being underage. No matter what boyish and romantic motives may have been involved in his initial attempts to get into army uniform, now he had discovered a cause and was unwaveringly dedicated to it. He had no doubt whatsoever that he was taking part in the defense of freedom for mankind against those dark powers which were hell-bent on trying to master the world. He'd had no qualms at all in picking off the Japanese soldier operating the machine gun; nor in actions on the way to Kokoda, and at Gona and Buna. Without any pangs of conscience, he had taken part in the slaughter of the Japanese. The pompous warning issued to him by the recruiting sergeant in Martin Place, Sydney—that he could be guilty of illegally killing the King's enemies—seemed something more suited to the soapbox cranks on Sunday afternoon in the Sydney Domain. He could not forget finding the beheaded corpse of a young Australian militia man near Kokoda, nor the human hands boiled in an iron pot for soup in a camp which a small party of starving Japanese had been forced to abandon—and the bodies from which those hands had been hacked. He had seen far too much of the way the Japanese lived, at times like savages; and the fact that on the body of one of them he had found a photograph of a family group, a dainty wife and two small children, had not tempered his attitude. But such first-hand experience of atrocities would be no help to him, should Hillyard inform Paine that he was underage. His lieutenant would be obliged to report the matter to the company commander, the information would be passed on and he would be withdrawn from active service, no doubt discharged, possibly dishonorably—perhaps even court-martialed and sentenced.

This fear was soon put at rest. Hillyard continued to reveal his inner panic to Rod, by his eyes alone. After having singled out Rod for reproof, he quickly sought to focus attention elsewhere, and Larry Donald fortunately provided him with a reason: he had been using his mess tin to pan for specks of gold. Outraged, Hillyard pointed out to Paine that in front of the platoon commander's very eyes, one of his men was committing an offense. A directive had been issued. Anyone removing any gold whatsoever would be charged. The gold belonged to those who lawfully held the mining leases, as did the dredging and processing plants which were out of bounds to all troops, whether Australian or American. They were to be left intact and untouched, even in the event of withdrawal, tactical or otherwise. In other words, the gold was forbidden fruit. And there was to be no "burnt earth" policy, as was being carried out by their unexpected allies, the Russians, in the face of the Nazi intruders.

Donald voiced the feelings of all four privates by muttering: "For crying out loud, what are we supposed to be doin' here! Fighting the Japs or protecting property for the bloody capitalists?"

Hillyard stiffened at what appeared to be insubordinate talk. Indeed, revolutionary talk. Paine, visibly irked by Hillyard, had to make at least some outward show of maintaining discipline.

"That's enough, Private Donald," he said.

Donald tipped the mud from his mess tin into the bottom of the weapon-pit and exchanged smirks with Mullen and Nugget.

All verbal communication was suspended for the next few minutes as several gray transport planes came over low to land, while on the ridges machine guns opened up at the few Japanese snipers who had not yet started to retreat into the mountain ranges.

Once conversation could be carried on again, Hillyard pointed to Rod.

"Er, Private Murray . . . " he began, only to be corrected.

"McKenzie," Paine interpolated sharply.

Hillyard's eyebrows shot up, but he let it pass—although not without having roused the curiosity of at least two of Rod's three fellow privates.

"McKenzie," Hillyard said. "I think I'm right in saying that you were a pupil of mine at one time."

Rod nodded and said flatly, "History." He would normally have added "sir" when answering an officer, but something inside him blocked it.

Hillyard was on the verge of saying it for him, but refrained, as if anxious not to provoke his former pupil. Instead, he said, "I'd like a private word with you, if I may." He turned to Paine.

Irritated even more by the intelligence officer, Paine said, "I'm hanged if I know what this is all about." It was something Nugget, Donald, and Mullen were also wondering. "But go ahead."

"A personal matter," Hillyard said, beckoning Rod up out of the weapon-pit, and at the same time supplying what sounded like a plausible reason. "I have something to tell him about a mutual acquaintance."

Like hell, Rod thought; he's just dreamed that up. But after Hillyard had led the way a short distance from the weapon-pit and stopped to speak, it turned out that the schoolmaster really did have something to impart.

"It's rather distressing, I fear," he told Rod. "You'll remember our sports mistress?"

"Miss Ross? Of course."

"I fear she is no longer with us. Level-crossing smash. She was in a bus returning to her camp."

Death had become almost an everyday occurrence to Rod, comrades cut down, dead Japanese, but learning about Mildred Ross jolted him. She had been all a beautiful young woman could be. And even though she might have been in the AWAS, to him she still belonged to the world he believed he and his mates were fighting for. It was a loss of something precious.

Rod felt incapable of adequate words. "I'm very sorry to hear about it," he muttered. As he spoke he was amazed to see tears in Hillyard's eyes.

Dropping his voice lower, the teacher said, "I think I can work out why you have called yourself McKenzie. And I think we can both be relied upon to keep our mouths shut about each other."

While the tears remained, the glare had vanished from Hillyard's eyes. Not only that, there was an unmistakable plea detectable in them. Rod was aware that he was in no position to turn down the terms Hillyard was offering, but it ran against his nature to enter into a compromise with someone who, in his eyes, was a contemptible rat, one whose predatory leanings had apparently remained unknown to the army.

So Rod agreed. "You'll be safe," he said bluntly.

Hillyard seemed satisfied by this, then fresh tears brimmed in his eyes and he had to swallow before he could speak. "You may or may not believe it," he said, "but Mildred Ross was a person very dear to me. We used to go hiking together, until she found me out for what I am."

In fact Rod *did* believe him; he had a glimmering of Hillyard's predicament and dilemma; in his eyes the schoolmaster could now no longer be regarded with quite the same contempt. Rod recalled how, when he was writing his lines on the blackboard in the schoolroom, Mildred Ross had spoken with a certain softness and understanding about him, saying, "Poor Dennis."

Quickly blinking his eyes clear, Hillyard turned away, leaving Rod to follow.

"What was all that about?" Nugget asked, once Rod was back in the weapon-pit. The two officers had moved on to speak to those manning the next emplacement. Nugget believed himself to be more entitled than either Fred Mullen or Larry Donald to ask such a personal question—although he had learned that Rod usually preferred to give nothing away.

With a wry grin, Rod sidestepped his question. "The last

time I opened my trap at the wrong time, he gave me fifty lines: 'The Enemy Listens.' "

"The bastard!" said Nugget, loyally taking it for granted that his mate had never deserved any such punishment.

"I remember—I couldn't spell 'enemy' properly."

"That's one thing the bloody war's taught you, then," Mullen commented drily.

Donald was strongly tempted to put two questions to Rod: how long ago was it since Hillyard had imposed those fifty lines and how old was Rod at the time?

To Nugget, who was twenty-two, Rod's age was no issue, even though he was curious about it. To Fred Mullen, it was a matter not to be pursued because, even though he claimed he was only sixteen at Gallipoli in 1915, he had been over the age limit of forty when he enlisted for the current war. Larry Donald's grounds for suspicion about Rod had originated six months earlier when he was attached part-time to the quartermaster at the jungle training center on the Atherton Tablelands. Rod had brought in one of his two pairs of boots for repair, but had reported that they had become too small—and so another pair of specially-made boots was requisitioned. Also, he needed trousers and shirts in a larger size. All of which had suggested that Rod could well still be a growing boy.

Donald was one of the unit's most ardent gamblers, a member of most two-up schools and all-night poker sessions. Now he moved a little farther afield from the weapon-pit to try his luck, crawling with his mess tin to a shallow in the ground which had a rivulet of seepage passing through it. He added a few specks of gold to those he had tipped into a tiny receptacle fashioned from foil that had been wrapped around a concentrated block of apricot in his field rations.

On the fourth day at Wau, he was busily panning at this position when he saw the platoon sergeant approaching by way of other emplacements, so he returned to the weapon-pit to be on hand for what he guessed would be a briefing about their next move.

Sergeant Pollock was another Middle East veteran, respected by all the men. Close attention was paid to what he had to say. The whole company was about to move forward. The Japanese might have withdrawn to mountain strongholds, but they would be attacking again. Wau, with its airfield, was a vital strategic position in a plan the enemy had apparently not abandoned: the push through to Port Moresby and from there to the Australian mainland. Pollock went on to say that the platoon had suffered casualties—one killed and now two down with fever: they would be evacuated to the Port Moresby hospital during the day. One was the section lance corporal, and it had been decided that his place would be filled by McKenzie, who was immediately promoted.

Pollock proceeded to the next position, oblivious to what he had left in his wake. Nugget thrust out his hand to shake Rod's, saying, "Put it there, mate—you'll be a general yet."

Mullen found it belittling to have anyone so comparatively young placed superior to him even by a stripe, although outwardly he doggedly adhered to what he claimed had been his policy as far as rank was concerned in two wars: "I started out sayin' I'd never take a promotion—and I never have."

As for Donald, he resented having been passed over for the vacancy, especially when it had gone to someone he believed to be underage for service. As he prepared to take up his panning again, he said, "Well, Lance Corporal—what's your first ever order going to be?"

The question was so facetious that it could have been ignored. Nevertheless, Rod considered it. By the time he had framed his reply, Donald was back in the nearby hollow.

"Stop panning for gold and keep your mind on the war."

Nugget winked approvingly at Mullen, who shaped his mouth into a neat puckered bull's-eye, as if Rod had achieved with words the equivalent to his prowess as a marksman.

Donald glowered in open resentment; and another of the many petty little battles within the one big war was joined.

7

From the day they found themselves in the same platoon of foot-sloggers, Rod had been shadowed by Nugget Bates. They had shared the same tent-fly for shelter, and Nugget had never complained about the fact that, because of his broken nose, Rod breathed noisily and heavily when asleep. For his part, Rod accepted that he had acquired a staunch mate and supporter.

Size had been a problem for Nugget, too, but in the opposite way to Rod. Although old enough to enlist, he was too short, and had been rejected when he first volunteered. Only when the conditions for acceptance were relaxed did he manage to succeed. Having adopted Rod as his special mate, he was naturally curious to know more about him; and so, despite Rod's inborn reticence, bit by bit he came to know more of Rod's background: about his parents and how they had become incompatible; about his mother's erratic and impulsive ways; about his affection for his peppery grandmother (Nugget had something of the same spirit and physical spryness); about Horrie Benson and the night work on the milk round; about Rod's fascination with the big ships of Sydney Harbor; and what might have happened to him for the first time in his life, but for the fact that just as the *Queen Mary* passed out through the heads, the *Queen Elizabeth* lined up to come in. (Rod was still a virgin; he had the Japanese to thank for ensuring that his romantic notion of preserving himself intact for Brenda King had not been shattered. With Nugget and others he had been in a Townsville brothel shortly before embarking for Port Moresby—but they'd had to vacate the premises in a hurry due to an air-raid warning.) Partly by being such a good and genuinely interested listener, Nugget so ingratiated himself that Rod came to trust him implicitly: he was even able to overcome his bashfulness and tell him about Brenda and convey something of his crush on her, at the same time revealing that she had a younger sister, Fran.

It hadn't been until the unit was back resting at Port Moresby, recovering from the Gona and Buna campaigns, that Rod had begun to write any letters—to the only people he could safely contact, his grandmother and Horrie Benson.

The first reply was from his grandmother, who wrote in a forthright style, as she spoke, and in a firm hand. She said how pleased she was to hear from him at last; she had been worried. The war news was better so "the local ladies are saying you must be giving them Japs hell." Then the bad news. His mother had received a telegram "out of the blue" saying that his father had been killed in action in the Battle of El Alamein. His mother was in a frenzy ("we both know what she can be like") but "it's an ill wind that don't blow somebody some good"; his mother was putting in for the war widow's pension, so "if she gets it she thinks she'll be set up for life and living in luxury." Meanwhile, his mother was still working in the munitions factory.

Shortly after this, there was a letter from Horrie saying he wished Rod and his mates would hurry up and win the war "because I'm getting worn out on the job." Rod got the meaning of this and had a laugh when Horrie went on to write that "Edgar's in the gun with one of the blackmarket kings after he had the hood of his Bentley for breakfast."

Nugget, one of seven children, was inundated with mail from parents, brothers, sisters, cousins, aunts and uncles; but was still keenly interested in the few Rod had received.

"What's the big joke?" he wanted to know when Rod laughed at Edgar's most recent gastronomic exploit.

Rod not only told him, but gave him Horrie's letter to read for himself, and so Nugget learnt that "your friend Brenda's young sister Fran is trying to get a job at the depot. Don't think her mum and big sister approve."

"Do you?" Nugget asked, looking up from the letter.

"Of what?" Rod asked.

"Young Fran getting a job at the depot?"

"She likes horses. She'd probably enjoy it."

"Sounds like she's quite a girl."

"She's a good kid," Rod said, busy thinking about Brenda again and wishing he could take up her invitation to write. He wondered if he might somehow manage to get a letter to her by sending it through Horrie, but that seemed to be an invitation for trouble. As did writing to his mother; she might somehow stir up things.

While Rod had seen evidence with his own two eyes that starving Japanese troops had resorted to a form of cannibalism, he accepted it as having been done out of desperation for food. The jungle was the real cannibal, hungry for human sacrifices through its blood-sucking leeches, disease-impregnating mosquitoes, poisonous ants, ticks and other pests; its swamps, its decay, its tangles of rotting vines which obscured the sun; the rain that left its intruders water-logged. And for the next six weeks Rod's unit lived within its infernal reaches; as its members patrolled and ambushed, they were themselves ambushed.

When Fred Mullen was in the Middle East, he had never missed a chance to claim that what he and his fellow in-fantrymen experienced in the Desert was nothing to com-pare with Gallipoli and the Somme. But of New Guinea, Mullen had no hesitation in saying: "At Gallipoli there was nothin' like the Somme—and on the Somme there was nothin' like this."

At the end of six weeks, the unit was withdrawn down the trails and tracks, partly on foot, partly by truck, to a rest camp near Wau for a few days to dry out and repair gear, to rest, and to catch up on letter-writing. While Nugget dashed off a dozen, Rod wrote just two, one to his grand-mother, the other to Horrie, belatedly telling them that he'd been promoted to a lance corporal.

There were no amenities such as a canteen or film screen-ings, but the Salvation Army padre supplied mugs of tea and coffee, and biscuits to go with them. Nearby was one of the richest gold-bearing creeks ever found, and so it was inevitable that some of the troops should be lured to it, including two members of Rod's section.

"You heard what Lieutenant Paine said about filching gold," Rod reminded them, looking in at the native-built hut the two shared.

Mullen looked cagey but Donald was cocky and defiant.

"We're restin', so it's no concern of yours how we spend our spare time." And then, with a clearly implied threat, he added, "If you know what's good for you, kid, you'll mind your own business."

Nugget realized what was worrying Rod; he now had no doubt that his mate was still well underage for active service, and he was fearful of the consequences of a showdown with Donald. So he encouraged Rod to forget about the two rebels and join him in another hunt, one not subjected to any bans, the pursuit of something which remained un-contaminated by any element of evil—butterflies. They had glimpsed some beauties sailing in and out of the jungle. Hunting butterflies was not unlike fishing. So Rod joined Nugget in fashioning a butterfly net, using wire, scraps from a torn mosquito net, and bamboo poles. The idea appealed to Rod, the chance to capture a legitimate souvenir that might appeal to a young lady as a gift.

And it seemed to offer a chance to allow his feet to share the break by leaving them bare. He had been suffering twinges lately and was well aware that the cause was not his boots shrinking but his feet having grown yet again. He felt that now, at six feet three inches, he might have finished extending upward, but that at ground level his feet were still spreading. As he set out with Nugget, his feet left some mighty prints in the mud, but not for long.

He was stopped in his tracks by a sharp, "Hey, there!"

As he sensed, the call was aimed at him—and came from the Medical Officer, Captain Boyle, who pointed at Rod's feet and called, "Get your boots back on! This ground's infested with hookworm larvae."

Rod remembered one way to pick up hookworm was through the soles of the feet, so he handed his butterfly net to Nugget while he slipped back to put on boots which had achieved a certain fame in the unit. The status of a secret weapon, in fact. They had left such massive prints on a track that an enemy patrol had stopped to examine them, as if they were in territory where a giant roamed. Their guard down, the Japanese set themselves up as an easy target, the entire patrol being wiped out by Owen gun bursts.

If Rod wore the boots without socks, they did not pinch so much, so it was with boots but minus socks that he rejoined Nugget, only to find that all members of the company had been called out on parade.

"What for?" Rod wanted to know.

"Blame an old friend of yours," said Nugget.

"What old friend?"

Nugget pointed to where Hillyard waited with the company commander, Captain Exton, Lieutenant Paine, and other platoon commanders, all looking distinctly peeved at having had their rest interrupted by a visit from the headquarters intelligence officer. The troops muttered loudly and shuffled about in protest at this intrusion on their hard-earned break.

Captain Exton, a small man, a former architecture student in his twenties, explained quickly that Lieutenant Hillyard was here on a matter that would appear to concern all of them. He didn't go into it but handed over the parade to Hillyard, who stood with a sheaf of papers in his hands, reminding Rod of how he had appeared before distributing marked history essays embellished with savage comments.

"I haven't a great deal to say," Hillyard began, "so I shan't be taking up much of your time. However, *what* I have to say is of the very utmost importance, particularly at this stage of our operations. It has come to my notice that we—and I speak of the battalion and do not single out any company—we are not taking prisoners."

He had to pause because a dark chuckle rose from a hundred throats.

Faced with a collection of equally dark grins, Hillyard raised his voice to become more admonishing. "May I remind you that it is not our policy to do away with prisoners, as it were, on principle. Indeed, as supporters of the Geneva Convention, we are duty-bound to treat all captives humanely. Not to shoot them out of hand. As has apparently been happening." He detached a document from the sheaf of papers and referred to it. "I have here a report made by a member of this company, who shall remain nameless. It would appear he could easily have captured a Japanese infantryman staggering toward him in a dazed condition. He claims to have said to the enemy, 'Good day, going some place?' And then, instead of effecting a capture, he promptly sent the infantryman on his way."

The assembled troops greeted this with a burst of cheering and laughter, identifying the culprit with cries of: "Shame on you, Billo!" and "Billo, you cad!"

To Rod, what Hillyard didn't seem to be taking into account was that Japanese sometimes tried to be taken prisoner because they had booby-trapped themselves—and when they dispatched themselves to Kingdom Come they took their captors with them.

Exton had to shout for order before Hillyard was left free to conclude.

"Yes, yes, it may well have its comic aspects. But it's not at all funny when you consider that we desperately need live, healthy prisoners to interrogate. Therefore what I am saying to you is—we want prisoners taken, not summarily shot. Thank you."

And then, as Captain Exton gave the order for the parade to dismiss, Hillyard called, "Is Lance Corporal McKenzie here?"

He did not need to look far.

"May we have a quick word?" Hillyard called.

"I'm comin' with you," Nugget said.

"No," Rod said. "I can handle him. Don't worry."

Hillyard went forward to meet Rod, who came to attention and saluted. Oddly, Rod had a sense of respect for the man that he'd never had before their confrontation on the Wau airstrip; and there was an almost kindly tone in Hillyard's voice as he said, "Stand easy."

He sorted through his papers and came up with what Rod saw was one of his own letters, written two days ago to Horrie.

He clenched his fists at his sides, a reaction Hillyard was quick to note—and quick to deal with.

"A censoring officer referred this letter of yours to me. To a friend called Benson. May I assure you that I have your best interests at heart, Lance Corporal—I hold myself in a sense indebted to you—but I have no alternative but to remind you that it is an offense to put anything in a letter in code."

"Code?" growled Rod, mystified.

Hillyard quoted from the letter. " 'Tell that boy of yours that Prickle-head is around the ridges and throwing his weight about.' "

Rod's mouth sagged in disbelief that Hillyard should need to ask his next question. "Who, may I ask, is 'Prickle-head'?"

"It's a sort of joke, y'see."

"But I don't see," Hillyard said testily.

Did this really mean, Rod asked himself, that Dennis Hillyard had no knowledge of his own nickname?

"Well, sir, it's a sort of private joke."

Hillyard seemed far from satisfied. "I'd be most careful in the future about introducing such elements into your letters. It might cause the censoring officer to mutilate them."

"Yes, sir."

"That'll be all then."

"Thank you, sir."

Rod saluted again, about-turned and marched off, easing into a walk as he reached Nugget, who waited anxiously with the butterfly nets.

"What's he on about?"

"Nothing really," Rod said, grinning. He told Nugget why he had been questioned.

"You mean he doesn't know?" said Nugget incredulously.

"Seems like it."

Nugget had a gurgling laugh, one that churned around inside him, making him shudder before it got out—and when it did, it was highly infectious. It proved the trigger for everything Rod had been holding back, and the pair of them drew attention to themselves as they rocked with laughter. Others wanted to know what the joke was about and joined in the laughter at the intelligence officer's expense.

The ensuing butterfly expedition was not successful. Rod and Nugget pursued some gorgeous specimens, but they were not expert enough with their nets to catch even one between them.

Meanwhile, others had been successful in a different way: Larry Donald and Fred Mullen had apparently reaped and hidden a small hoard of the forbidden gold.

Next day the rest period was over and the unit moved back up along the tracks and trails to its former position in holes in the lee of a jungle ridge, and the patrols began again.

8

The jungle was never devoid of menace, never completely
silent. It dripped and rustled and whispered. The enemy,
though, could be utterly soundless, except when attacking
as if hunting wild pigs, yelling war cries, shooting haphaz-
ardly, blowing bugles, waving flags (which Australians and
Americans alike greatly prized as souvenirs) and shouting
in English to the Aussies to give up and die for their martial
overlord, Field Marshal Tojo.

There were, however, isolated places in jungle-clad
mountain areas where, in contrast to the prevailing sinister
atmosphere, Rod had discovered a cathedral-like hush and
calm. In the naves and transepts of moss forests, where
overhanging branches, tree trunks, and ground alike were
covered with pale and darker-green moss. On the forest
floor, the moss could disguise bogs into which a man could
sink suddenly to his waist or to his armpits, although where
Rod had been the ground moss simply provided a carpet
that deadened the sound of footsteps and made walking a
luxury. After the unspeakable mires through which he had
dragged his feet, these were oases of peace. He had seen

the occasional butterfly fluttering soundlessly through them, although the depth of the silence was such that Rod was prepared to hear a minute creaking of ornate wings, the way he used to hear the sound of rusty hinges coming from seagulls' wings on the foreshores of Sydney Harbor.

After another two months of constant skirmishing with the enemy, the company was put on reserve for a few days to allow the men to recover from exhausting day and night patrols. A big swag of mail arrived, a wad of letters for Nugget, two for Rod. One from Horrie, the other from his grandmother. Horrie's was short; he seemed to be tipping off Rod that the letter he last received had been cut about by the censor. The one from his grandmother was as cheery as ever, saying how pleased she was to know he had been promoted and that some of his ancestors had been NCOs. She went on: "I have been honored by a visit from your mother. Her Ladyship says she has waved goodbye to the demon drink, so let's hope she means it *this* time. She is worried about you, where you are, not hearing from you. I didn't tell her anything, but thought you ought to know, as she just might have turned over a new leaf. Like the leaves on the tree, we're all capable of that, provided the wind is strong enough."

Nugget, meanwhile, failed for once to read through all his mail. He was running a temperature and fell asleep. He refused to report to the M.O. for fear of being sent back down the line and parted from his mates.

Many of the men were passing their rest time by making souvenirs out of malleable metal and perspex from a Japanese bomber which had crashed nearby, shaping model war planes, signet rings, paper knives, miniature Australias. Nugget had brought his butterfly net back from the rest camp near Wau, and seeing it reminded Rod of the sort of souvenir he would like to send away. A butterfly. To Brenda. He recalled a day when the King and Murray families had been on a picnic to the National Park, and he and Brenda had chased butterflies together. He had used his sunhat to catch a red and brown Painted Lady. And now he remembered a place here, in neutral territory, a moss forest where he had glimpsed some prize specimens gliding and courting.

Along with Nugget's butterfly net he took his rifle and ammunition. Although the tracks he followed were assumed to have been cleared, booby traps were sometimes overlooked; this called for a sharp watch with every footstep. Rod's boots were pinching his feet even more these days, and almost every step was accompanied by a twinge, a reminder that he needed a bigger pair.

Once he reached the moss forest and entered one of the naves, he thought of the thick pile carpet in the apartment from which he had seen the *Queen Mary* and the *Queen Elizabeth* pass each other. On his way to vantage points overlooking Sydney Harbor, he had not always hurried past St. Mary's Cathedral, that landlocked ark made of sandstone blocks. Inside the soaring structure he had found himself amongst tall stone pillars, and now he was among arboreal pillars, tree trunks covered in moss and encircled with vines. Here there were many naves and many transepts, and at the end of one of the latter he glimpsed a butterfly, a flash of electric blue in a rod of sunlight penetrating the overhead entanglements of branches. He put down his rifle and readied his net, waiting for another butterfly.

When another did appear, throwing off emerald light, he moved toward it, skirting around the moss-covered pillars and through frail curtains of hanging creepers. Rod assumed that he was quite alone here; this was not the case, but he remained unaware that he had the company of another human being, just as that other person remained equally unaware that he was not alone.

Obscured from each other by intervening tree pillars, by creepers hanging like strands of weft waiting for weavers of jungle tapestries, the two were in pursuit of the same errant butterfly, which suddenly tumbled upward to skim far out of reach through the cathedral-like arches, leaving both pursuers standing cheated—until they became aware of each other's presence, some twenty of Rod's paces separating them, possibly forty paces if measured by the other.

Rod might have been prepared to find an Australian here, or perhaps an American, but he was stunned to discover that his fellow hunter was a Japanese soldier, a small, docile-looking man who appeared to be in his middle twenties, with a very thin straggly beard on an otherwise almost hair-less face, and wearing a soft peaked cloth cap.

They faced each other with raised butterfly nets, ready now to be employed as frail weapons of attack or defense.

At no time since he had been serving in Papua and New Guinea, on the way to Kokoda, at Gona and Buna, from Wau to his unit's present position, nor when attacking the enemy strongholds at the village of Mubo, had Rod been so long in the known company of a living Japanese man. He had seen the open eyes of many dead Japanese, but until now never those of the living. The dark eyes which confronted him showed unmasked fear, yet no hostility; rather a readiness to observe a truce. A truce, because in their harmless hunt for butterflies they clearly shared an interest that set them apart from the world of armed conflict around them. For the very first time, after having come to accept that all Japanese were inhumanly fanatical and bes-tial, Rod realized that among the enemy there might just be fellow human beings. This prevented him from taking

any precipitate action against the Japanese butterfly hunter—
and then, as if to remind him of the basis on which he and
his enemy stood face to face, a large butterfly with flashing
red embellishments on velvety black wings appeared almost
midway between them and began to weave an airy scroll.

Lowering his net, the man bowed to Rod, then gracefully
gestured to him to try to capture the handsome black and
red specimen, at the same time speaking in accented but
clearly-enunciated English, his words deadened by the moss
surroundings.

"After you."

At first Rod was so knotted up physically and mentally
with astonishment that he was incapable of taking up the
invitation, and the butterfly swiftly sailed out of reach. Other
butterflies appeared, and both Rod and the enemy soldier
pursued them, the latter more a manikin than a full-grown
adult in comparison with the Australian. Their hunt led
them in and out of the naves and transepts, moving away
from each other, then coming closer again, until at almost
the same moment they each succeeded in making a capture.

The Japanese soldier held up his lilac and gold prize
within the fabric of his net and, again enunciating clearly,
said, "Very beautiful."

Rod held up his, an emerald specimen, and nodded his
agreement.

"You will come here again?" the soldier asked.

Rod found himself answering, "I might."

The soldier bowed, then started to back away. Rod also
began to edge back—until, when he lost sight of the man,
he ran out of trust and turned and raced to the transept
where he had left his rifle, grabbed it, and kept on at a run
out of the region of the moss forest, along the jungle tracks,
arriving breathless at his camp.

Nugget was drowsy but brightened at the sight of Rod's prize, echoing something of what the little Japanese soldier had said of his own catch: "What a beauty."

Due to the daily dose of the anti-malarial drug, atebrin, everyone's skin had a yellow tinge, something which was more pronounced with dark-haired men like Nugget; now that his skin was pale because of fever, the yellow was greenish. He still refused to let Rod ask the M.O. to see him. Rod, meanwhile, mentioned nothing about his strange encounter with a Japanese soldier. Not that he dismissed it from his mind. Far from it. He lay awake that night trying to decide whether he should report it. In the morning when he woke, the problem confronted him again and he realized how he would have to act.

It was the company's third and last day in reserve. Rod asked to speak to Lieutenant Paine alone. First he revealed that his boots were becoming too small and that he needed larger replacements.

"So put in a requisition," said the platoon commander, irritated that someone like McKenzie, who knew about such procedures, should waste his time.

"I know, sir," Rod said. "But there's something else." And he gave an account of what had happened in the moss forest, somehow feeling he was guilty of a betrayal.

Paine, no longer impatient, asked, "Was he alone?"

"Definitely."

"And he speaks English?"

"Yes, sir."

"Could account for some of those 'Die for Tojo' yells we've been hearing."

"It could," Rod granted, although the Japanese soldier had impressed him as being anything but a warlike type.

"They'll certainly be interested in this back at battalion headquarters," said Paine, seated cross-legged on the ground at a box which had survived an air drop of rations and was now serving as a desk for his papers and field telephone. "This could be just the chance your old schoolmaster has been looking for."

Rod felt that he was being reminded of his betrayal. As Paine spun the handle of the field telephone, he told Rod he might want him again soon, so Rod called in nearby and lodged his requisition with the quartermaster corporal together with outlines of his feet. As for when the request would be met, according to the corporal it might be months, it might be never, it could be a boot at a time, maybe a full pair, probably not two pairs: "Could even be a pair and a half."

The quips fell very flat with Rod.

Back with Nugget, whose eyes had become glazed, and voice hoarse, it was apparent Rod had something on his mind.

"What's the matter?" Nugget wanted to know.

"Nothing."

"Mate, when you say 'nothin',' that really means there *is* somethin' doin'."

As Rod considered confiding, Nugget said, "I've been havin' some rare ole dreams." This wasn't anything altogether new. Even without the help of a fever, Nugget had dreamed that the Germans had destroyed the Sydney Harbor Bridge. But his latest effort knocked Rod sideways nevertheless. "Apparently the Germans have sunk the *Queen Mary* and the *Queen Elizabeth*."

"Since when?" Rod demanded, shattered.

"Since I dreamed it." And sensing Rod's dismay, he added, "Just a nightmare, mate—nothin' to it."

But Rod still couldn't help but feel that Nugget might have had some insight into an immense double calamity, like that suffered when the mighty British warships *Prince of Wales* and *Repulse* were dive-bombed to death by the Japanese off the Malayan coast a few days after the attack on Pearl Harbor.

Before Nugget could try to talk him out of his concern, Rod was called to the company commander's tent.

"Like I guessed," Nugget said breathlessly, "something's up."

Outside the tent, Captain Exton and Lieutenant Paine had a map spread on the ground. They asked Rod to pinpoint where he'd encountered the Japanese butterfly hunter, so with his forefinger Rod took them along the tracks to the moss forest.

Exton, who wore the white-purple-white ribbon of the Military Cross, referred to notes on a message pad as he spoke. "This situation could provide us with an opportunity to capture an intelligent Japanese soldier and through him discover something specific about enemy objectives and strategy, which at the present time remain somewhat obscure. In the first instance, McKenzie, it is suggested that you try to establish a rapport with the Jap by continuing to hunt for butterflies in the same forest area." He jabbed his forefinger at the location on the map Rod had identified. "In view of the risk involved, headquarters instruct that it should be carried out only on a voluntary basis."

"It's okay by me, sir."

"Good. Once you've got to know the fellow, report back and we'll decide where to go from there. Give it three days for a start."

"Yes, sir."

"Have a good rest tonight and check out at daybreak."

Nugget was in a deep sleep under their tent-fly, so Rod was able to assemble his kit and rations without having to face up to questions about where he was going and why. When he left at daybreak, Nugget's skin was shiny with sweat and he was murmuring in delirium. Rod felt the fever must be reaching a climax and be about to break.

The moss forest location could be reached by a number of tracks, so Rod took a different route than on the previous day. He spotted some recent Australian bootmarks; this did not surprise him as the area was under constant patrol.

For much of his life Rod had been a rather solitary person (he had thought it a laugh when he heard one of the old ladies at Ultimo holding forth on the subject of only children and claiming that they were invariably spoiled brats), so he did not feel lonely or isolated when on his own. He had done solo patrols, and stints by himself at remote observation posts. Once back in the moss forest and jungle, he chose a vantage point by a moss-covered rock, which gave him a wide view of the many naves and transepts.

He settled down behind the rock to watch, listen, and wait. Like an occasional falling star, a vine broke and slithered down to the moss floor. The only other movements were those of tiny lizards, jerking forward in stops and starts—until, after nearly half an hour had passed, the first butterflies appeared. They came alone, in pairs, sometimes more, like magic little flags, silken and highly colored, with lives of their own, flags free to flutter as the whim struck them, without winds or masts. Then the mosquitoes arrived, one or two for a start, and silently, even when they appeared in small clouds. He found that leeches had attached themselves almost invisibly to his gaiters; one penetrated below the gaiter on its way to sample his blood. The day passed without the Japanese butterfly hunter or any other living person appearing, so he prepared for the night. It would be an ordeal; he felt his noisy breathing might give him away. Darkness brought the fireflies with their phosphorescent lights, floating and hovering as if threatening to search him out. A host of green starboard lights, helping to remind him of Nugget's nightmare about the two *Queens*.

In the morning, as he refilled his water bottle from a stream below the point of entrance to the naves and transepts, making sure to insert a purifying tablet, he smelled what seemed to be a whiff of coffee, but then he was in the midst of jungle odors that often gave rise to comparisons, the sour smell of stale milk being one of them, bringing with it recollections of the milk and ice depot and the round with Horrie.

It was early the following afternoon, when he glimpsed a shadow move in the distance, a dozen long forest naves away, then vanish, only to reappear nearer. Rod, with his rifle ready, was able to identify the Japanese butterfly hunter, moving towards the place where they had met, at the same time using his net to try to capture tumbling glitters.

Rod waited until the man was still nearer; then, after putting down his rifle and picking up his butterfly net, he moved out from behind the moss-covered rock so that he could be seen and identified. Which, presently, he was.

The man again bowed, although from a greater distance than at the first meeting. "I am most pleased to meet you again."

It was as if he was saying that, having discovered themselves to be members of a brotherhood dedicated to the pursuit of living gems, they were no longer obliged to treat each other as enemies. In the face of such an assumption, Rod's sense of treachery was all the more acute.

A green dazzler, like the one Rod had snared and taken back to camp, sailed down and gyrated between them, then began to seesaw toward one and then the other, tantalizing them as they stood poised with their long-handled nets, taunting them as if intent on taking no one side in their conflict. The butterfly's flight took on an upward spiral, and at the top of its ascent it hovered, wings beating, momentarily marking time—and then, without warning, because the blasts came after the destruction had been done, the butterfly disintegrated, a tiny flag torn to shreds by a burst of bullets fired from behind the soldier.

Rod fell to the moss floor as the little man stood horrified, staring behind him to see what Rod had already seen—a small detachment of steel-helmeted Japanese marines advancing with weapons raised and aimed.

The man looked back to the Australian soldier, the anguish and consternation on his face leaving Rod in no doubt that he had known nothing of the presence of this detachment.

Nor had Rod known of the presence of another detachment, a platoon from his own unit.

There were reports from behind *him* now, and smoke canisters landed in front of the Japanese marines, exploding into leaping tendrils which swiftly expanded to a billowing white cloud.

"Get down!" Rod yelled, and the soldier, too, fell to the moss floor, and as the submachine guns rattled and the hot lead bullets scorched and skimmed above them, the innocent and the betrayer lay bound together in another way, each having been used as a decoy by his own side.

Before the smoke cleared, the Japanese man had been taken prisoner and Rod had been guided away, his rifle and gear retrieved for him by members of the platoon which had been sent ahead of him and had already been in position the morning he had arrived—explaining the fresh bootprints on the track and the whiff of coffee.

At company headquarters, to which Rod and the prisoner were hastened back, Captain Exton waited with other officers, including Lieutenants Paine and Hillyard.

"Our boys had you well covered all the time, McKenzie," Exton assured him.

"So I found out," Rod said. "Did they know those Japanese marines had followed the prisoner?"

"No," his platoon commander answered. "Nor did the prisoner himself, apparently. He was observed trying to slip away on his own yesterday and warned about it. When he made a second attempt today, he was allowed to go—but followed."

"You did well," Exton told Rod.

"Particularly well," put in Hillyard. It was he who had advocated the plan to send McKenzie to the moss forest on his own.

The prisoner was present, left standing a distance away near Exton's tent, blindfolded, hands tied behind his back, his arms roped to his sides. That Rod could ever feel sympathy for an enemy soldier, for any Japanese, would have been something he would have ridiculed vociferously until forty-eight hours ago. Now he felt disgust at himself and the officers for the way the poor little bugger was being treated. He had been searched, of course, and his papers were held by Hillyard, who now added to Rod's distress.

"Our instructions are to arrange for the immediate escort of the prisoner to the mainland, for the fullest interrogation. You'll be in charge."

"Of what?" Rod asked, sensing something he was not going to be ravingly happy about.

"Of the prisoner. You'll be escorting him. Probably to Brisbane."

"Brisbane!"

"Quite a reward, eh? A trip back to the mainland."

"But I don't want to go back to the mainland."

"You-don't-want-to-go?" Hillyard said with exaggerated incredulity, spacing his words, while Exton and Paine, realizing what was behind Rod's attitude, started to look most uncomfortable.

"I want to stay here—with my mates."

As Exton, Paine, and the other officers knew, Rod was trying to say that he would consider himself to be deserting his mates if he left like this. There were a few wayward comrades in their ranks, hard-case rascals such as Larry Donald and Fred Mullen, but in the main the members of this fighting unit were bound together in their dedication to a cause like disciples of some crusading religious order, many of them lean and haggard before their time, wearing jungle-green uniforms in place of monkish garb. Rod looked to Exton and Paine for support, something noted by Hillyard, who became spokesman for a higher authority.

"I'm afraid you have no choice, Lance Corporal. This decision was made at operational headquarters."

As Rod saw, both Exton and Paine had to agree, openly showing their dislike and resentment toward the zealous intelligence officer, who now took Rod by the elbow. He flinched as if the schoolmaster's touch might carry some contamination. Hillyard steered him to a point out of hearing of the prisoner—and the other officers.

"Like yourself," he said, once they had stopped, "the prisoner believes he has been duped by his comrades."

"Duped?" Rod repeated, not too sure of its meaning.

"Let us say—used."

"You can say that again!" Rod muttered feelingly.

"Therefore you have that in common. It could well be that the prisoner may tell you things, take you into his confidence. Be a ready listener. You never know what valuable information you might pick up."

Having been used as a betrayer, Rod felt that he was now being forced to play the role of an informer.

Hillyard was about to lead the way back to Exton and the other officers when Rod said:

"Could I ask you a question, sir?"

Hillyard braced himself as if in readiness to back into a protective shell. "Go ahead," he said with great wariness.

"You're in intelligence, sir—you could know about such things. Has anything happened to the *Queen Mary* or the *Queen Elizabeth*?"

For a moment, Hillyard reacted as if Rod might be attempting in some curious way to get back at him for that fifty lines punishment he had dished out two years ago; then he saw that the lance corporal was in earnest.

"The reason I ask, sir, is that my mate—Private Bates—had a dream, y'see. About the two *Queens*. That both of them got sunk by the Germans."

"I've heard nothing to this effect, I assure you. The two *Queens* sunk? A dream?" Hillyard managed a dismissive laugh, partly one of relief: he had been prepared for a very awkward question from the lance corporal. "Believe me, we've enough rumors to contend with, without dreams."

But Rod's mind was not yet fully at ease as he received a briefing from Captain Exton and was told to pack his gear and be ready immediately to backtrack to the airfield at Wau, with the prisoner, there to pick up a plane for Port Moresby.

Since being brought back with the captive he hadn't been to the tent-fly and he was concerned about Nugget. Much more concerned when he found his mate's bush bunk empty.

One of the two who shared the closest tent-fly called out to him: "The M.O. heard he was crook so came up for a look-see. Had him taken back to the field hospital. Called in the stretcher-bearers."

Hell, thought Rod, Nugget must have been worse than he'd assumed. "What did the M.O. say?" he asked.

"A bad dose of dengue—and that he needed lookin' after."

As he assembled and packed his full kit, it upset Rod that he would have no chance to visit his mate. Twenty minutes later he was on his way in a jeep, with Hillyard and the prisoner, whose name, it transpired, was Ohara—Hiroshi Ohara—a not uncommon Japanese surname, but it had a Hibernian association that caused some amusement as the fact spread around the camp.

"A bloody little Irishman!" Fred Mullen laughed as he and Larry Donald saw the party leaving the camp. Unlike most others, who had a good deal of respect for young Rod McKenzie, they were delighted to see him go. Maybe if he got caught up in the leave and transit depot in Brisbane, he might get lost there.

This was something which Rod was already worrying about. Once in the clutches of such depots, there was never any guarantee that a soldier would get back to his original unit. A member of the company had gone to the mainland on compassionate leave when his wife was gravely ill following the birth of a child. The child was said to be nearly walking by the time its father returned. Nor had this possibility failed to occur to Dennis Hillyard. In fact, it was on his very strong recommendation that McKenzie was appointed the prisoner's escort. With a little luck, Hillyard might never have to worry again about what damning beans his former pupil might spill.

9

"You'll need to be on your toes all the time," Hillyard warned Rod at the Wau airfield at first light next morning, after staying there overnight. "The prisoner may well try to take his own life. Shame of capture. Failing that, he might try to take yours."

Prickle-head would probably prefer the latter, Rod mused, as he and the Japanese soldier boarded a U.S. transport, one of the fleet still flying between Wau and Port Moresby.

The real danger proved to be from Australians and Americans who clearly would have taken great pleasure in killing the prisoner. They raised fists and guns at him, keeping Rod busy warning them to clear off.

Ohara was no longer blindfolded, but his wrists were bound in front of him and his feet hobbled, so that he had to move in quick mincing steps—to the amusement of on-lookers, which angered his escort, who held two ropes, one attached to Ohara's body, the other to his ankles. Beside the lance corporal, the Japanese soldier was tiny, child-like. Rod sensed that Ohara bore him no grudge, but rather looked to him for protection, which he received not only on the Wau airfield but also when they changed planes at Port Moresby to a four-engined American Flying Fortress bound for Townsville, and there transferred to an RAAF twin-engined Hudson for the leg to Brisbane.

Both escort and prisoner wore tropical issue drill and cotton clothing, and so had a taste of the cold at higher altitudes as they crossed the Owen Stanley mountain range. At Port Moresby, Rod asked for blankets; he draped one over Ohara and the other around his own shoulders.

Eating and drinking presented Rod with no great problem, as he simply fed his prisoner; but nature's calls were not so easy. On his own, Ohara managed to pass water but when it came to sitting on a latrine, Rod had to untie his hands and embarrass Ohara and himself by standing there with his rifle.

At the two stops, and inside the planes before the engines were started, after which conversation was impossible, Rod found his prisoner keen to talk, and he discovered that although Ohara was proceeding to Australia under armed guard, it was not his first visit.

"My father shipping manager. We live in Sydney at Darling Point," he told Rod. "I go to school for one year, Sydney Grammar." Rod knew where this was. A college opposite Hyde Park. He had passed it many times, including one morning when he had run all the way from Ultimo to Mrs. Macquarie's Point to see the *Queen Elizabeth* anchored where the *Queen Mary* had been the previous evening.

Rod learned this on the ground at Port Moresby, before a wild Australian bulldozer driver came charging at Ohara, waving a jack knife and shouting, getting the Japanese war cry "Bansai!" mixed up with the name of a Gaelic spirit who had terrified his ancestors. "Banshee! Banshee!" he yelled.

As they waited inside the Flying Fortress, in metal seats near the bomb bay, Rod gathered that Ohara had been a student of economics in Tokyo and was engaged to be married. All Ohara's possessions had been taken from him after his capture, but a small wallet had been returned and was now in his tunic pocket. He asked Rod to extract it and open it out. It enclosed a tinted photograph behind plastic which had become blurred in tropical heat and humidity: he saw a gentle-looking Japanese girl in a traditional kimono, her hair arranged high and glossy. Ohara told him she was accomplished in the art of flower-arranging. Tucked into another compartment of the wallet, Rod glimpsed a square of silk.

At Townsville, their second stop, there was a delay in changing planes, and Rod learned that the prisoner's father had been transferred to New York and had taken his son on trips, including several across the Atlantic to Europe. Rod's curiosity was really roused. What ships had he traveled on? How could Ohara ever forget? The *Bremen, Ile de France, Queen Mary*.

In New Guinea Rod had met Middle East veterans who had been transported to Suez in the company of thousands of men on the first of the two great *Queens*, but until now he had never spoken to anyone who had sailed on her before the palatial furnishings, drapes, chandeliers, paintings, and other items, which made her a floating luxury hotel, had been removed in the process of refitting her as a troop ship. Rod found himself asking many questions.

He had been informed by Hillyard that once he had handed over the prisoner, he himself would be interrogated.

He sensed that Hillyard had deliberately returned the wallet to Ohara as it might encourage him to talk. Which it had indeed done. Yet everything Rod had discovered seemed pretty harmless, unlikely to alter the course of the war in any way.

About the time he expected the Hudson to be nearing Brisbane, the plane began to bounce, soar, then drop alarmingly. An orderly struggled back from the cockpit to shout that because of heavy thunderstorms in the region they would be bypassing Brisbane and going direct to Sydney.

It did not matter to Rod whether he handed over the prisoner in Brisbane or Sydney, although the change of destination raised other issues, good and bad. By going to Sydney he would be able to visit those he knew; but to get back to New Guinea, he would face having to go through the leave and transit depot there, and it was notorious for delays and for sending men to units other than their own.

After a hard landing at Sydney's Mascot airport, they disembarked into the chilly darkness of a mid-May night, Rod going first and helping Ohara to follow him, not bothering to hold the two rope ends since even if the prisoner did try to bolt, his hobbled feet wouldn't get him anywhere.

Two military policemen appeared, both wearing MP armbands and peaked caps, one a sergeant who greeted them by dragging away their blankets and tossing them to his companion. The two arrivals shivered in the cold, although in Ohara's case it was as much from fear. The sergeant took hold of the two loose rope ends and, after flicking them as if they were reins, he yanked hard on the one attached to the prisoner's ankles.

Ohara's feet were pulled away from under him and he fell hard on the asphalt surface with a stifled cry of pain.

As he lay there, unable to get up, the sergeant drove his boot into the prisoner's frail buttocks, snarling, "Come on, ya little yella mongrel, get up!"

Moments later the sergeant himself was trying to get up. Rod had learned his unarmed combat well. With what seemed to be little more than a jab with the edge of his hand, he struck at the bullying MP's Adam's apple. The sergeant went down on one knee, and would have crumpled onto the asphalt, had he not managed to steady himself with his hand. Though groggy, he knew what had happened to him. He tried to bawl, but the best he could manage in his temporarily weakened state was a hoarse threat.

"You'll be on a charge for this."

"On what grounds?" Rod inquired evenly as he placed his hand under Ohara's armpit and lifted him back onto his feet, feeling his violent trembling, like that of a maimed petrel he had once found flapping about on a jetty on the Harbor foreshore.

"Striking a senior non-commissioned officer," the MP sergeant claimed, getting some of the bully back into his voice.

"You assaulted the prisoner. It's my duty to protect him."

"I've got a witness," went on the sergeant, ignoring Rod's grounds.

But the junior MP was quick to shake his head and state his position. "I didn't see anything."

"He chopped me!"

"I repeat—I didn't see anything."

In such a situation Rod would have assumed that even if two military policemen were not in agreement, they would, so to speak, close ranks. Apparently he'd had the good fortune to find a pair severely at loggerheads.

Abandoning his threat, the MP sergeant pushed himself

up onto his feet. "I never thought I'd live to see the day when an Australian soldier defended a bloody Jap!"

"Neither did I," said Rod, aware of the irony, even though he had yet to come to terms with the profound change of attitude his involvement with Ohara had brought about.

"Follow me! Unn, doo! Unn, doo!" the sergeant commanded, stepping out with his contrary colleague, and making no allowance for the fact that the prisoner could only hobble. "Unn, doo, tree, tor!"

"Give us a chance!" Rod protested, and to prevent any argument or further bullying, he trailed his rifle in his left hand and wrapped his other arm around Ohara's tiny waist and carried the prisoner on his hip, despite the heavy load of his full kit.

An MP van was waiting, and the sergeant told Rod to climb into the back with the prisoner. He had orders to deliver them both to headquarters, Victoria Barracks, Paddington. Rod demanded the blankets back, and once inside the van he draped one blanket over Ohara's shoulders and the other around his own as before. They were padlocked in and shared a bumpy ride through streets steeped in gloom, with Rod reflecting on his own audacity. He had often wanted to thump an MP, but this was the first time he'd had a genuine excuse for doing so. Wait till he told Nugget!

At the convict-built Barracks, scene of many men shackled by chains and ropes, the hobbles were removed from the prisoner's ankles, but his hands remained tied at the wrists. Rod formally handed him over when the duty officer signed for him. Before Ohara was taken over by the duty corporal, he bowed deeply to Rod and said, "Thank you."

Rod was so moved that he reached out and gave Ohara

a pat on the shoulder, something that neither the duty officer nor corporal seemed to approve of. Ohara fumbled with his tied hands to try to extract his wallet, but before he could do so, he was abruptly marched away.

Rod himself was escorted to the office of a senior member of the headquarters intelligence staff, a Major Pender, who accorded him a much different greeting from the one received at the airport.

"Do sit down. You must be damn weary after all the way you've come."

It occurred to Rod that there were, like Japanese, good and bad Australians, but before he sat he insisted on carrying out his assignment to the letter and took the sealed envelopes from his haversack, handed them to the major and waited for a signature on the receipt form he also put forward.

Having received that signature, he took the chair in front of the desk. Major Pender rang a small bell, then opened the envelopes, spilling out various possessions taken from Ohara, then extracting a small sheaf of papers. He clipped on a pair of rimless spectacles.

As he began to peruse the papers, there was a knock on his door, and a most attractive soldier appeared, a dark-haired AWAS, the major's secretary.

"Iris," he said, "I wonder could you arrange some tea and sandwiches for this young gentleman? He's had a long journey."

"Certainly, sir," said the AWAS, giving Rod a warm smile before leaving the office. The trouble was, she reminded him of a honey-haired AWAS and he felt saddened all over again for Mildred Ross.

The refreshments duly arrived, served on a tray covered with a lace doily. Lighting his pipe, the major puffed as he read, reminding Rod that he still carried his grandfather's old pipe. It had become a keepsake. The trip had been so sudden and swift it was hard to believe that he was back in Sydney, free to see his grandmother. And Horrie. And possibly Brenda. Not necessarily in that order. As for his mother . . .

The major looked up and began to ask questions, going through all that had happened from when Rod had decided to go butterfly hunting on his own. He kept nodding, puffing smoke, murmuring, "Good, good"; "Go on, go on." He took notes, and when Rod revealed that Ohara had told him that his father had been a shipping manager in Sydney, he went to a filing cabinet, unlocked it, brought a folder of documents to his desk and found a reference to Eizo Ohara, confirming all that Rod had been told.

"Our people assumed he was gathering information. Much the same went for the entire Japanese diplomatic and business communities here. They gleaned a detailed knowledge of the city of Sydney and Port Jackson—layout, currents, depths, and so forth. As we discovered last year when their midget submarines got into the harbor."

Rod knew about that. It had happened when he was still training on the Atherton Tablelands. Fortunately, neither of the *Queens* was present that night; by then they had started transporting Americans across the Atlantic to Great Britain.

At this point, a Japanese-speaking captain who had been interrogating Ohara elsewhere in the building, came to Pender's office with the small square of folded silk which Rod had glimpsed tucked into the prisoner's wallet.

"The prisoner has asked that this be given to his escort," said the captain, glancing at Rod. "As a token of his esteem. What is the situation, sir?"

"Let's have a look at it," said Pender, taking the square of silk. He unfolded it carefully on his blotting pad, revealing a tiny picture made of parts of butterfly wings—a green sea, purple mountains, blue skies, and a red bird in flight, all delicately cut out, mounted on thin cardboard backing, and surfaced with cellophane. The captain said, "The prisoner told me that he made it for his fiancée, but brought it along with him when he hoped to meet Lance Corporal McKenzie again—to show him what he did with the fruits of his butterfly catching."

"This is quite exquisite, don't you think?" Pender said, holding it up to Rod, catching some of the light from the overhead bulb on its iridescent surface.

"It's pretty good, all right," Rod said, remembering that he had left his emerald butterfly pinned to one of the uprights supporting the ridge pole of the tent-fly he shared with Nugget.

The captain told the major that the battalion intelligence officer, Lieutenant Hillyard, had included this item in the wallet because he felt it might have some special significance, the nature of which McKenzie might glean.

Major Pender asked Rod what he made of it.

"It looks like a souvenir to send home. Like some of our boys make model planes out of scavenged metal and perspex."

"I'd say you were right," the major agreed. "And I shouldn't think there'd be any harm in you having it. That's if you want it?"

"I do," Rod hastened to reply.

So Pender refolded the silk square just as carefully as he had opened it out, then handed it across to him. Then the captain informed Pender what the questioning of Ohara had so far revealed.

It would appear that Ohara had not been as distressed about his capture as he might have been. In fact he seemed pleased to have escaped from his O.C., a Captain Astashi, who was apparently a boorish martinet. More importantly, it would seem that the Japanese higher command had not given up hope of counterattacking strongly from their Mubo bastion, sweeping back through Wau, then on to Port Moresby, and there setting up a springboard for another attempt to gain a foothold on the Australian mainland. Batches of fresh troops, including marines, had been brought down the coast by barge from the pre-war trading posts of Lae and Salamaua under cover of darkness. As a student, Ohara had been flattered when asked for his views of the economic strategy of his country regarding Australia; it would appear that Japan, like the United States, saw Australia primarily as a source of food, manufactured goods, and munitions. And if Japan could not have Australia for these reasons, then it would try to cut it off from America.

As the captain started to leave, Rod asked that his thanks be relayed to Ohara for his gift. The captain referred this to Pender with a questioning look and received a nod of approval.

Alone again with Rod, the major observed, "As a race the Japanese are extraordinarily artistic. This comes out in odd ways—in their ammunition, for instance." Rod looked at him uncomprehendingly. "Surely you've seen some of their ammunition?" Pender said.

"Stacks of it."

"Then think about it. Beautifully designed and finished— and artistically packed."

So Rod thought about it and had to agree. Until now he had never regarded anything Japanese as artistic.

Pender went on to make further observations, including one about Rod's unit and the lonely force of which it was part. "You're a remarkable lot of fellows, you know—no more than a mere brigade and a couple of commando companies, yet the only allied forces facing the Japanese anywhere on land in the Pacific theater."

This only made Rod feel all the more anxious to be back with his comrades as quickly as possible.

"I daresay Hillyard was right in pushing for you as the escort, the prisoner did open up his heart to you. Nevertheless, I somehow gather that you didn't volunteer for this chore."

"Definitely not, sir."

"But you *did* volunteer to go back to the moss forest to make further contact?"

"Oh, yes."

"Damn risky thing to do, if you ask me."

Rod's reaction was to do something he did with a certain expertise: he shrugged.

Pender checked through his notes, then looked up and removed his spectacles. "We'll have you bedded down here in the Barracks for the night. In the morning, I suggest you go across to the leave and transit depot in the showgrounds. The duty officer will give you all the necessary authorities. You'll need some warmer clothing."

"I've got a pullover. All I need is a pair of heavy trousers— and maybe a great coat."

"I should think so. It's getting damn chilly. You must have quite a bit of leave in the kitty."

"Forty-six days," said Rod; he'd checked this. "But I won't be taking anything like all that."

"No?" questioned Pender.

"I've got to get back," Rod said, with a touch of breathless desperation.

"Of course you do," Pender hastened to say, with real understanding in his voice. Rod's dedication to the cause and his loyalty to his comrades were overwhelmingly apparent. Pender himself had been a young officer in the Great War, then a successful lawyer, but had found himself over-age for active service, so he'd had to settle, reluctantly, for a desk job. "If there's anything at all I can do for you, McKenzie," he said, "please don't hesitate. Call here. Ask for me."

"Thank you very much, sir," Rod said.

There and then, he did have a request to make of the major, a key man in intelligence. Seeing him poised to speak, Pender said, "What is it, McKenzie?"

"It's about the *Queen Mary* and the *Queen Elizabeth*, sir."

Rod was ready to see Pender react with grave concern at their loss, but instead he looked deeply puzzled. Until Rod described his mate's nightmare.

"Good God, that was a nightmare and a half! To my knowledge, both ships are still hale and hearty. Let's see what we can find out."

He phoned a friend in naval intelligence, put his question, listened, nodded, grunted, expressed his thanks, replaced the handset of his phone, and beamed at Rod. "No need to worry. Apparently both ships have just made successful Atlantic crossings with full quotas of American troops."

Rod could also have mentioned his need for new footwear, but at this moment his boots weren't giving him the slightest reminder of the problem they had become. Away from the heat, the humidity, and the jungle streams, and after cooling hours flying at high altitudes, his feet were no longer swollen, as they had been almost constantly in New Guinea. His boots felt quite comfortable, even though as recently as thirty-six hours ago he had been limping along the jungle trails.

10

A violin was being played out the back as Rod stepped into the quartermaster's store. The tune was heartrendingly soulful, but Rod had no ear for it as he stopped in front of the counter and faced tiers of shelves piled with clothing and equipment. A brass bell was chained to the counter beside a notice: ONE LOUD RING ONLY. So Rod grasped the handle and rang once.

The playing stopped and presently Sergeant Josef Falbermann appeared with his violin and bow. He subjected Rod to a suspicious appraisal over the tops of small round spectacles. All who came here were potential thieves and looters, out to obtain issues to which they were not entitled and to try to take him down personally.

"You rong?" he said querulously in a thick Middle European accent.

Rod's reply was to hand over the authority from the duty officer at the Barracks. The quartermaster sergeant scrutinized it carefully. He had been a member of a touring Austrian classical string quartet, marooned in Australia at the outbreak of war, and had been interned with his fellow musicians and manager, until, after a boring six months, he had decided to point out to his custodians that he had been born in Lima and that the Peruvian passport which they had confiscated had in fact been issued by a friendly nation. He was released from internment camp, only to be drafted into a base unit of the army. He took his army posting almost as seriously as his music, to which he devoted at least four hours of practice a day.

Rod produced his Record of Service Book in readiness for new entries to be made, and said that he was taking some leave before going back to his unit in New Guinea. He needed heavy trousers and a great coat.

Falbermann extended his bow to gauge Rod's measurements, judging him for size, giving the bow a twirl to indicate to Rod to turn around. He disappeared for a few minutes and returned with the trousers, dropping them on the counter in front of Rod in a way that conveyed a professional respect for the item of clothing but a certain disdain for the intended wearer. As he went off again, Rod wasted no time, removing his boots and jungle-green lightweight trousers to try the heavy pair for size. They were short in the leg, but they would do. Falbermann came back with a huge great coat which enveloped Rod as if he had stepped into a heavy khaki bear costume.

As the quartermaster sergeant entered the two issues in Rod's Record of Service Book, instead of putting his boots on again, Rod lifted them from the floor and placed them on the counter. "I could do with a new pair of these," he said.

Eyeing them warily, since boots of this size merited respect, Falbermann examined each in turn, then said, "Vy a new pair? These boots haf much life in them yet."

"They've grown too small," Rod explained.

"Boots do not *grow*—especially too small!"

"What I mean is—my feet seem to have grown."

"Oh, yes?" Rod was aware that a new light shone from the quartermaster sergeant's eyes, a gleeful light, as if he had uncovered someone trying to get the better of him. "I suppose you expect me to tell you zat I do not haf your size in stock, huh?"

"Usually they're not in stock. I have them made to measure."

"And while you vait, you vill haf to go on leave, huh? Extra leave." Without giving Rod a chance to reply, he went on, shaking his forefinger. "And it vill be my fault. Vell, my friend, you cannot put that one over me." The wagging forefinger was joined by its immediate neighbor, both of which were thrust upright close to Rod's face. "Two days! In two days I haf them here from the makers. I send the order to them by runner, so if you sink you use me to wangle extra leave, you make the big mistake."

"Honest," Rod tried to protest. "You've got me wrong."

"Wrong?" repeated Falbermann. "I see through you. And let me tell you somethink more. It is no use putting in an order without a certificate from the M.O."

"Why the M.O.?" wailed Rod, as if he had to get proof of his sanity before he could get new boots.

"I require the certificate from the Medical Officer stating zat these boots are not big enough for you, because your feet haf grown."

Falbermann dipped his steel-nibbed pen into an inkpot and completed the entries in Rod's Record of Service book, and returned it after blotting the ink dry.

Rod checked in his rifle and all the gear he would not be needing for the duration of his leave. He had an initial pass for five days and had drawn the huge sum of ten pounds from the nest-egg in his Pay Book, one that already far exceeded any sum he had ever thought he would possess.

The quartermaster sergeant continued to look very pleased with himself as Rod replaced his boots and departed, taking up his violin and playing a lively piece, as if his instrument had become one of those homecoming fighter planes Rod had seen doing victory rolls.

The Medical Officer's hut was just a step away. Maybe, thought Rod, he should get that certificate . . . but he decided not to bother. After their overnight rest his feet felt even more comfortable.

If he cut through Surry Hills he would come out near Central Railway Station. Autumn leaves on deciduous trees reminded him that it was about this time of the year he had raced barefooted all the way to the harbor to see the *Queen Elizabeth*. Two years ago plus one month. He glimpsed gray warships and drab freighters at anchor in the harbor now. He hoped to get along to its foreshores later. Now that he was on leave, although he felt he was sneaking time off while his mates were left to handle the war, he could not help being a bit elated.

He noticed changes. Since it was Saturday, the traffic was light anyway, but because of gasoline rationing the appearance of some of the vehicles had altered dramatically, especially private cars. Many had steel frames fitted overhead to contain gasbags, making them look like airships with outsize gondolas; others had charcoal burners and cylinders fitted to their rear ends, as if equipped with incinerators. Even in the back streets, the proportion of those in uniform to civilians was much higher—and he saw many Americans, including marines, resting here, he surmised, after the battle on Guadalcanal in the Solomon Islands.

There were posters everywhere calling on men and women to enlist for the three services. Others exhorted civilians to invest their savings and earnings in war loans and victory bonds. Wherever a Japanese man was depicted, he was an ugly, toad-like being, and Rod, who'd had much the same image in his mind, particularly after seeing so many dead ones, now regarded what he saw as exaggerated caricatures portrayed by ignorant artists.

It was too late in the morning for Horrie Benson to be at the milk and ice depot, but Rod dropped in nevertheless, surprising the clerk in the accounts office, then going to the stables to say a quick hullo to Edgar. The clerk told him the horse had bolted again one morning when planes from an American aircraft carrier buzzed Elizabeth Bay. Rod felt he should have brought the horse something special to munch, a chunk of motorcar hood, maybe.

Steam laden with the smell of hops came from the brewery near Central Railway Station as it helped to cope with the thirsts of a fighting nation and its visiting allies, although no beer had reached as far as Rod's unit as yet—not that this concerned him. He reveled in the smooth pavements and it wasn't long before he was at the pub corner in Ultimo. Rod thought it unlikely that Horrie would still be having his nightcaps on the house, but he entered by way of the public bar just in case.

Bert Heffernan, the publican, was charging the bar tills with small change in readiness for the day's guzzling. After a hard look, he recognized Rod, but no longer treated him as a minor; he was a serving soldier and Heffernan was a veteran of the Great War, one who justified his illegal after-hours trade as a service to the drinking public, officially denied by unfair laws.

Horrie had left half an hour earlier, but how about having a beer on the house?

Rod bashfully owned up to never having had a beer. Even with Nugget and others in Townsville, he still hadn't tried, although a playful attempt had been made to force some of it down his throat. He had seen too much of it being swilled by his parents. He accepted a lemonade instead, and the publican decided it was an occasion to start a little earlier than usual himself, and had his first whiskey of the day.

"Matter of fact," he told Rod, "I didn't touch the grog meself until my last few months in France. Here's to you, son. Horrie's been tellin' me about you. Must be rough up there. The Jerry was no saint, but he was a 'uman bein', had some honor. With the Nips, you're up against animals. Fanatical wild bloody animals!"

Rod let the publican prattle on. It was true, the Japanese troops were fanatics, especially those who had to be literally burnt out of bunkers made of earth and trunks of coconut trees. Peaceful outposts such as Gona and Buna had become the scenes of horrific slaughter. As far as Rod was concerned, at the time he was in these places, the Japanese had been animals. He gave no hint now of his rethinking and mellowing, and Heffernan took this silence as confirmation that Rod agreed wholeheartedly with his views.

"Another lemonade?" Heffernan asked.

One was enough thanks; Rod was on his way home.

"Sorry to hear about your dad," the publican said.

Rod remembered that his mother had often claimed that his father spent more time at the corner pub than at home. No mention was made of her so as he started in the direction of home, he wondered whether he should call on Horrie first, to try to find out the local situation; but by now the milko would be asleep in bed.

Nothing seemed to have changed—until Rod reached the horse-trough. It was dry, its bottom covered with rubbish: empty bottles, sweet wrappings, used cigarette cartons, including American brands, a dented celluloid doll's head, a sock, a broken pram wheel, scraps of newspaper. He could see what had happened. The inlet pipe had corroded and had been pinched and sealed off.

He was astonished to find the gate of the terrace cottage was not only shut but that it swung in from the footpath smoothly and quietly when he opened it. Then he saw that the front door, which had been in need of attention for as long as he could remember, now boasted a coat of fresh paint. It was shut, but the metal knob turned and the door, too, swung in on renovated hinges. For a moment he wondered whether he might have come to the wrong address, but there was the brass number in front of him, 5, newly polished. He hadn't knocked; he thought perhaps he should, even though the door was half open. But as he raised his knuckles he saw something white hanging from that bane of his life, the hat-stand. As his eyes swiftly adjusted to peering into the gloom, he saw that it was part of a naval cap with a gold and silver emblem and a shiny peak, one he recognized as belonging to an American naval petty officer.

Back at the scene of some of his more spectacular attacks of clumsiness, he felt the affliction threatening him again. And so he backed away. No sound whatsoever came from within the house. Yet this was Saturday morning, the previous Friday night invariably having been marked by partying and drinking, and the next morning by his mother's snores and flubbers. He forced himself to tread softly and carefully as he'd had to do hundreds of times on jungle tracks and trails. Once clear of the cottage, he stepped out. He would come back to see Horrie. In the meantime, there seemed to be only one place to go, to the haven he had always found waiting just outside Parramatta.

———

At his grandmother's house, the neglect that had greeted him in the horse-trough was on a much larger scale. The front patch of lawn, which he had mown almost every time he came here, was ankle-high, weeds taking over the garden, the hedges untrimmed and unruly. The shack, neat and cozy as it had always been, had only a few windows, and now curtains had been drawn across them. The front gate was padlocked.

At first he thought his grandmother must have moved. Or gone into a home. Yet she had been too sprightly for that, despite her asthma. Then he saw the letter-box jammed with mail, the ends of some of the envelopes beginning to yellow. So he started to empty it and found his own letter, the last one written to her, stamped and duly initialed by a censoring officer. An elderly man from the cottage next door appeared at his side.

"You're the grandson, aren't you?" he said.

Rod nodded, already gleaning from the sympathetic look on the neighbor's face what had happened.

"My deepest condolences. She was always so kind an' bright. Laughing she was, just told a friend a joke, then lost her breath, an' one of her attacks came on."

"When?" Rod managed to ask.

"Nearly a month ago. Didn't you know?"

Rod shook his head, sending the streaming tears zigzagging over his cheeks.

"Must be a terrible shock for you. I'm sorry. Come along— the wife'll make you a cup of tea."

At first Rod allowed himself to be led, then pulled away. Suddenly he found himself with something to settle on behalf of the old lady.

"Thanks all the same," he said, "but I'll have to catch the first train back to Sydney."

He was so emphatic that the neighbor didn't try to persuade him otherwise. He started out for the bus stop so as to reach the Parramatta Railway Station as quickly as possible, then turned back, but only to retrieve the last letter to his grandmother. Before he reached the bus stop he had ripped his letter, the envelope and its contents to small pieces which he dropped into the storm-water ditch.

The early winter darkness was starting to fall when he returned to Ultimo, glad to have brought along his great coat. The names of the streets and the railway stations had been removed, and the street lighting reduced to a few heavily-masked overhead lamps. It seemed that only tricklets of electricity were being used, until Rod began to hear the radios, dramas vying with quiz shows and musical programs from house to house along the streets.

Home was browned out, too, but as the front door was ajar a little, a faint glimmer of light reached the passageway from the sitting room at the front, and from here came the sound of a radio tuned to a popular quiz show, the whooping voice of the compère, the cheers and applause of the studio audience, as contestants proved the genius of the human mind by winning prizes for such remarkable mental feats as remembering how many days in a year.

On the footpath, Rod braced himself, almost as if going into action against the enemy. He opened the front gate and with two strides reached the front door, which he pushed inward; then a few steps in the passageway to the open door to the sitting room, where he suddenly appeared in the frame, stooping, because he still wore his slouch hat.

The only source of light here, other than the glow from the dial of a large new radio console, was from a shaded standard lamp. A man in his early forties, wearing a navy-blue cardigan, looked up from where he was seated in an easy chair, his expression very stern, as if Rod might be some passing interloper who had strayed in off the street—until his mother, in the other easy chair, let out a cry.

"Rodney!"

She was drinking coffee, and the cup and saucer would have fallen from her hands if the man had not been so quick to reach out and take them from her.

"Rodney!" she cried again, struggling up out of the sagging upholstery of her chair, while her male companion, realizing this was the young son home from the war, reached in another direction to turn down the quiz show.

As his mother came toward him, her arms held out ready to embrace him, Rod remained in the frame of the door and uttered the accusation over which he had been brooding ever since leaving his late grandmother's vacant home.

"Why didn't you tell me Grandma was dead?"

"How could I? I didn't know where you were."

"You could have told Horrie Benson," said Rod, using the flat of a hand to keep his mother at arm's length, refusing to allow himself to be embraced by her.

"What help would that have been, for heaven's sake?"

"He knew how to get in touch with me."

"But I didn't. And I didn't know about Horrie, anyway. Or whether you were still alive—or gone like your father."

"Maybe I should mosey along," said the American.

"No, Hal—I want you to meet my son. Rodney, this is Hal Frobish—he's a very good friend of mine."

Frobish, a man with crinkly fair hair touched with grey and a crinkled forehead, as if he frowned a lot, through care for others rather than ill-humor, extended his hand to Rod, only to be rebuffed.

"I can see that," Rod said cuttingly.

Then, realizing that he had gone too far, there seemed nothing else for it but to get out of the place, so he turned round and strode out, leaving both front door and gate open behind him, storming past the cluttered horse-trough and along the street. Only now did he start to notice things in the images he had gathered while in the sitting room. It had been unusually orderly; his mother composed; the Yank didn't seem a bad sort of a chap. Perhaps he had jumped to a wrong conclusion: the Yank certainly looked offended— and his mother distressed—by his remark.

Maybe Horrie could shed some light on the situation. As he headed for the Benson home, he passed an air-raid warden on patrol, checking that brown-out rules were being observed. His presence at first seemed to Rod ridiculous, until he remembered that it was only a year since Sydney had been shelled by a Japanese submarine off the coast, and that ships were still being sunk.

Horrie was awake and up and preparing to have, at this late hour of the day, his breakfast, while the rest of his family had their evening meal.

The Bensons, Horrie, his wife and five children, warmly welcomed the towering young lance corporal and treated him as if he had been holding the Yellow Peril at bay single-handedly. They assumed he was enjoying a well-earned break, but Rod was anxious to set this straight: he had left his unit in the New Guinea mountain ranges temporarily and much against his wishes. He felt he was in no danger of breaching security by telling the Bensons how he had been detailed to escort a Japanese prisoner of war to Sydney.

Spider, on behalf of all five kids, was eager to know more. Had the Jap tried to committ hara-kiri and kill himself? No, Rod told him; in fact his main problem had been to protect him from being done in by Australians and Americans.

"I'da had a go, too!" said Spider. Then: "How about Prickle-'ead? 'As 'e killed many Japs?"

"Don't think so," Rod said. "He's a headquarters man."

Rod was tempted to extract his wallet and take out his gift, the small square of folded silk enclosing the tiny picture made from butterfly wings, but he didn't feel up to becoming embroiled in trying to point out that not all the Japanese were necessarily like those toothy, monkey-faced monsters in the war posters.

Horrie finished his breakfast, and his wife shepherded the five children away so that their father and Rod could be together. Horrie was genuinely sorry to learn that Grandma McKenzie had passed on; he hadn't heard, but then why should he? Rod then revealed what had happened earlier in the day at the terrace cottage.

"Yeah," Horrie said, "I knew about it. It was somethin' I was wonderin' if I oughta let you know by writin' to ya. Except I wasn't clear on the situation, not until Bert Heffernan tole me."

Rod made it plain that he would welcome any enlightenment Horrie could provide.

"Well, if you hear it from me, you'll get the truth. Your mum was in the pub just about every evenin' after-hours, and when news came through your dad had been killed, she went on a binge and wanted Bert to give her credit until she got her war widow's pension. She got so rotten that her own mob dumped her, an' when she left the pub, she fell down in the street. Seems this Yank fella come along, he'd been at one of them socials for servicemen ole Mrs. Riordan an' her mob run at the Catholic school. He picked her up, found out where she lived, then took her home an' left her safely inside. Next day, he come back here to go to mass at the church and looked in at your place to see how your mum was gettin' along. He's at Garden Island, working with the navy. Well, she wasn't too good, as you'd expect, but he looks after her. Nothin' ulterior as they say, just a decent sorta fella. Since then, she's sworn off the grog. Bert reckons he hasn't sighted her in the pub since, not once. Of course, the Yank himself don't drink, but he's not a wowser though."

So this accounted for the change he had seen in his mother, and for the orderly state of the cottage. Rod felt more ashamed than ever of the way he had burst in, made his accusation, and then left.

"She's a character of an old girl is that Mrs. Riordan," Horrie chuckled. "She's takin' the credit for it."

"For what?"

"Your mum goin' on the straight an' narrow. Says it's divine intervention in answer to her prayers."

This forced a grin out of Rod.

Becoming serious again, Horrie went on, "Seems like they've got to be very much attached to each other."

Rod had gleaned something of this in the very short time he had been with them.

"Seeing as how he's on the level, it seems the old girl don't see nothin' wrong with him staying with your mum in his time off." Then he changed the subject. "What are you up to tonight, anyway? Like to give me a hand on the round for old time's sake?" Horrie paused to cock an ear and make sure his wife was still putting some of the kids to bed. "Things have changed. I'm in danger of being stuck with the dregs. The town's full of Yanks and they're cream-ing off all the talent, so maybe you'd do best by goin' to the local hop."

"What local hop?"

"Things have looked up around these parts since you was here last. Every Saturday night there's a dance in the school hall—to give the boys in uniform somewhere to go. *And* the girls. That friend of yours, that Brenda, she's always there, helps organize 'em."

"What about Fran? You said in your letter she was trying to get a job at the depot."

"She did. Stable-girl."

"What about her mother? And Brenda? You said they were against it."

"Had to accept it. Her dad was home on leave, and he said she could leave school and take the job if that's what she wanted. She's hoping to join up with the Women's Land Army—but not for a long while yet—she's much too young. But bloody cheeky all the same."

Horrie said this with some feeling, and Rod grinned as he asked, "In what way?"

"Reckons for a married man with kids, I do too much canoodling."

"Well, you do, don'tcha?"

Horrie chuckled. "Maybe I do, maybe I don't. What about you? Goin' to the dance? I often look in at the hall on my way to the depot."

Rod became serious again, thinking about it, then he shook his head emphatically. "No, I've got to go back home."

11

This time, even though it was his home, Rod knocked before entering, giving two loud raps on the new tan paint, then turned the handle and opened the door, hearing a Saturday sports summary from the radio in the front sitting room.

He closed the door firmly, deliberately making a noise, just in case the knocks had not been heard. They had. As he hung his slouch hat next to the petty officer's cap, his mother appeared in the passageway.

"Thank goodness!" she cried. "I thought you'd run away on me again!"

As he started to rid himself of his pack, he couldn't fend off his mother's embrace, even had he wished to; she hugged him for the first time in years; the small boy in short pants now a youthful giant in uniform.

She helped him out of his great coat, then led him into the sitting room, where Hal Frobish waited. There was no need for any apology; simply by returning Rod had said enough. Frobish extended his hand again and Rod accepted it and received a warm paternal shake as his mother switched off the radio. As all three felt their way, Rod learned that Frobish was a professional navy man, a widower without a family, five years older than his mother, who was now thirty-seven. He was a cryptographer and had been on the aircraft carrier *Lexington* which had been sunk a year ago in the Battle of the Coral Sea.

His mother had been allotted a temporary allowance pending the award of a war widow's pension, but as she fondly revealed she would not be going ahead with the claim because she and Frobish planned to marry. She was still working; she was now an inspector in a war clothing factory, having changed jobs to break with the company she had been keeping from the munitions plant. In the evenings she was taking instruction from the local parish priest in the Roman Catholic faith, Hal's church, and hoped to be received into it within a few months.

Where they would eventually live depended, like so much else, on the progress and outcome of the war. Hal might retire and settle in Australia, or they might live in the United States. Wherever, Rod would always have a home. Did he have any idea what he would like to be after serving as a soldier? Surprisingly, he had a very definite ambition, something which had its origin when he had spoken to the apprentice from the Cockatoo Shipyards. Much as he would like to travel on ships, he had no desire to work on them. He could only see himself in some menial role, such as a steward or ordinary seaman. Much more interesting and constructive to have a hand in the actual building of ships. The war was still at a critical stage, but post-war plans were being laid; members of the services were being encouraged and advised by education units toward careers to take up once they were out of uniform. Nugget Bates had made up his mind; he would go back to his job as a mechanic in a garage, but study at night, pass some examinations, then try to open his own service station.

It was clear to Rod that Frobish had given his mother something which had hitherto eluded her, protection and understanding. It was a shame his grandmother had not lived to see this. The old lady might have been outspoken about her daughter's shortcomings, but she would have accepted the transformation with joy. She'd had a saying which made allowances for such a change: "They say monkeys are full of surprises, but monkeys have got nothing on human beings."

"You must be hungry," his mother said at last. Yes, for the first time since reaching Sydney, he really was. His emotions had been running so high that it had not been, as he and Nugget had sometimes envisaged, an orgy of favorite meals the moment he set foot back on the mainland.

How about an old favorite dating back to when he was in short pants—fried bread, bacon, eggs, tomatoes, and chips? Rod's mouth watered so much it was almost as if it was in the grip of a flash flood. And so, as his mother went to the kitchen, Rod and Frobish were left together, conversing as fellow veterans, despite the age difference between them.

When Frobish described the sinking of his ship as "just one of those things," Rod sensed that the petty officer had no great prejudice against the Japanese, something which was presently confirmed. As a permanent navy man he had visited Japan and liked the country and its people. He believed that warmongers had gained control and instilled a crazy ideology into the minds of the masses; yet this did not excuse countless acts of barbarism and cruelty. Frobish was not at all surprised that in Hiroshi Ohara, Rod should have met a civilized fellow human being. There were many such Japanese, although you could be lynched for suggesting this.

The meal was delicious, and after it Rod took his pack to his room. Everything was in place, including his model *Queen Mary*. Seeing it made him wonder how Ohara had been faring. Major Pender had assured him the little Japanese soldier would be well treated and sent to a prisoner of war camp once he had been fully interrogated. Rod wondered what would have impressed him most, apart from sheer size, if, like Ohara, he had experienced a peacetime trip on the great liner. Ohara had been amazed to find a hothouse and nursery for plants and flowers on board, all tended by a sea-going gardener.

It was still mid-evening, so Rod decided to take up the suggestion made by Horrie and drop in at the dance at the school hall. His mother urged him to go, saying he was bound to meet young people he knew. But as he took his slouch hat and great coat from the passageway and set out, he was conscious there were things he had not revealed to his mother and her kind friend. In particular, that he had not enlisted under his own surname.

At the school hall no one would know that he had enlisted under a name other than his own, but many would be able to work out, if they so cared, that he was underage for military service. It needed only one person to act as an informer and he would be picked up by the military police and taken in for questioning. Imagine what tolerance and understanding he would be treated with if he happened to be sought out by an MP like the thug of a sergeant at the airport!

Reaching the blacked-out school hall, which hummed within like a huge hive, he paused in the way he pulled up on patrols to satisfy himself that there was no immediate danger ahead or to ascertain the nature of the danger he sensed. It was almost as if he were leading his section, his hand held up to signal those behind him to halt and freeze, to watch and listen and barely breathe.

As he debated with himself whether it was worth the risk to enter the hall, a torch was flashed at him and a voice came from the darkened porch, that of the man keeping the door. "Come on in, soldier. Everyone's welcome. No charge."

So he stepped forward, passed the beaming doorman in the porch, pushing through heavy dark drapes into the brightly-lit interior, the hum heard outside now a roar of talk and laughter. He seemed to be confronted with a sea of young faces, girls from their teens to their early twenties, young Australian and American soldiers, sailors and air-force men. His size alone made him conspicuous, quite apart from his yellow atebrin-tinged skin and recent short-back-and-sides haircut. Several instruments were being tried out on the stage where the headmaster had once stood to praise Prickle-head Hillyard for volunteering. A four-piece ensemble was made up of two pupils he recognized from the last school dance, the other two a gray-haired lady pianist and an elderly trumpeter with Great War medals flapping on his chest from full-length ribbons. They all looked in his direction.

He was again in a mind to retreat when, coming toward him, he saw someone he took at first to be Helen King, mother of the two sisters, only to realize that it was Brenda, looking very grown-up, with high-heeled satin shoes, makeup, and something of her mother's air, smart walk, and smile.

He was aware, of course, that he himself was different both physically and in mental outlook from the gangling, clumsy, uncoordinated, and largely inarticulate fourteen-year-old he had been when he last came to a dance here, wearing sandals borrowed from Horrie; but he was not conscious that the change in him was so marked and capable of making such an impact on others, until he saw it in Brenda's hazel eyes.

Her voice glowed, too, as she greeted him by telling him that everyone in the hall knew why he was back home from New Guinea. Thanks to Horrie, who had dropped in here on his way to the milk and ice depot, Rod's fame had preceded him. Apparently he had risked his life by escorting a highly dangerous Japanese prisoner of war from the jungle battlefront.

Rod had to laugh at Horrie's embellishment. "That prisoner would have to be one of the least dangerous Japs in the whole Pacific," he told Brenda.

"I don't believe a word of that," she scoffed politely, just as her mother might have done, yet looking a more attractive Brenda than he had ever seen or imagined.

"You're staying, I hope," she said.

"Well, now that I'm here . . ."

"Let me take your hat."

He had forgotten he was indoors and removed his hat to have Brenda hang it on one of the pegs on the wall, alongside other slouch hats, sailor's hats and caps, air-force forage caps, while he hung up his great coat.

The ensemble started to play a two-step.

"You're asking me to dance, I hope," she said.

"I haven't improved," he warned her.

"Let's try," she said, guiding him.

His feet, which could tread as softly as the paws of a cat on jungle tracks, were tightly confined in their army boots, but he managed to avoid actually stepping on her satin shoes, despite some stumbles. One of the worst being when he spotted a petite girl waving madly at him as she danced with an Australian sailor and recognized Fran.

"How does she like working at the depot?" he asked Brenda, realizing as soon as he had spoken that it was an inane question. Of course Fran must like working there, it was what she wanted to do, to look after the horses.

"We don't talk about it actually," Brenda said, dismissing what was obviously a touchy subject. "We can't wait until she's old enough to join the Women's Land Army."

"What about yourself?" he asked.

"As soon as I'm eighteen I'll be joining the AWAS. Sixteen months to go unfortunately. In the meantime I'm working in the Hospitality Bureau in Martin Place, sending servicemen to homes for dinner and parties. You'd be amazed at the number of people who phone or write in, saying they'd like to entertain one, two, sometimes even half a dozen." Then she changed the subject in time to the music as they swung in a different direction. "I never got that letter you promised."

Since the reason he hadn't taken up her invitation to write was also a touchy matter, he excused his lapse by saying, "I'm not much of a letter-writer."

Fran insisted on partnering him in the next dance, even though he warned her, too, that she could be exposing her feet to some crushing treatment.

"Don't worry," she said cheerfully. "You won't be able to do much harm. I've had horses' hooves trampling all over them."

"How's Edgar?" he asked.

"Edgar's a good boy, considering the company he keeps."

Realizing she meant Horrie, Rod burst out laughing and looked down to see Fran giggling helplessly. As had happened when he was dancing with Brenda, former school-mates, girls and boys who were now young women and young men, welcomed him home, some insisting on shaking his hand. But when the dance with Fran ended, he found himself confronted by a contemporary who had regularly run second to him in the sprints and long jumps at the school sports. A resentful Harry Downer, thick-set and pugnacious, now an apprentice boiler-maker.

"No wonder you had it all over on me," Downer said.

Rod, not clear what Downer was getting at, looked blank. Besides anything else, he was suffering from a feeling of unreality: three days ago he had been deep in jungle and mountain ranges, with no prospect of returning to the mainland for aeons—if ever.

"You put your age back," Downer claimed. "You didn't start school till you was nearly ten. You had three years on the rest of us at least."

It was as if, after having had a certain presentiment of danger ahead when outside the hall, Rod had walked into an ambush. The youth confronting him, even though they were in fact almost the same age, was still a boy by comparison with Rod, trained and tried as a jungle fighter. He had slaughtered human beings, even if at the time he had been convinced that he was taking part in the extermination of some deadly and crafty form of vermin. In Rod's eyes, Downer was naive and foolhardy, daring to taunt someone who was virtually a trained killer.

Part of that training, something which had enabled him to survive, was to know when to withdraw—and he wasted no time in doing so now, not only ignoring an insolently demanding question from Downer, but feeling curiously protective towards schoolmaster Hillyard—"Anyway, what's the latest you know about Prickle-head?"

Brenda came rushing over, fearful there might be some repetition of a fight that had broken out on an earlier Saturday night over an altogether different issue, whether an airman or a sailor had prior claim on one of the girls. Fran stood by, not knowing what to do or say, although ready to fly at Downer for insulting a brave young soldier.

"It's time I went," Rod said, snatching his slouch hat from its peg on the wall, then his great coat.

"Aren't you going to see me home?" Brenda asked quickly.

"Can't wait, I'm sorry," he said, assuming that she would be staying on until the dance finished.

"I've had enough," she said, and as he moved towards the heavy dark drapes that blacked-out the entrance, she hurried back to her chair by the wall to pick up her handbag and woolen stole.

Since the matter of Rod's age had been brought up, as they headed toward her home, Brenda sought to put Rod's mind at ease. "We all realized you got in underage," she said. "But Mother told us it was your business, and so did Father when he came home on leave."

It was a relief to Rod to know this, although he was fast making up his mind that he would have to cut short his leave and try to get back to his unit.

Believing he was indebted to Major King, and therefore that he should make some polite inquiry about him, he asked Brenda where he was posted.

"He was wounded in the Middle East. In an attack by German dive-bombers. So he's been posted to ordnance headquarters in Melbourne. Mother seems to think he'll be promoted to Lieutenant Colonel—and that he'll try to make the army his career after the war's over."

Again, as they walked through the empty browned-out streets, her high heels tinkling at nearly twice the time of his hobnailed clumps, he had the feeling that Helen King spoke through her elder daughter.

"Are you doing anything with your coupons?" she asked, as they approached the gate of her cottage.

"Coupons?" he asked.

"For clothing," she said.

"Haven't got any."

"Oh, but you're entitled to some."

"What for?"

"You must have coupons to buy clothing."

"I've got all I need," he said, meaning that he was issued with everything he required.

"What about pajamas, for instance?"

"Don't wear 'em."

"But you can get coupons for them, even if you don't need them. From the quartermaster's stores. And if you don't need them, I'd be very happy to have them. We have an awful time trying to make our ration go far enough. Only a hundred and twelve for a whole year. For a frock you have to hand over thirteen—I've got my eye on one I'd like to buy in time for next Saturday's dance."

Rod thought to himself that he wouldn't be around these parts next Saturday. With luck—and he realized he would need plenty of it—he might even be back with his unit.

And then, just in case he might think that by asking him for his coupon ration, she might be doing something illegal or unpatriotic, she said, "Father gave me all of his."

The feeling that the Brenda he had idolized was turning into a younger version of her mother persisted—that is, until they reached the cottage gate, when she stood on tiptoes, pressing her lips so softly and warmly on his that what he had so long imagined was made real again.

Yes, he would go to the QM Store at the showgrounds

leave and transit depot the next day, Sunday, and call back in the evening—with, he hoped, an issue of clothing coupons for her.

Although Rod continued to believe that he must cut short the brief leave he had taken and try to return without delay to his unit, he slept comfortably that night, back in his own bed for the first time in sixteen months. Both his mother and the petty officer were asleep in their rooms when he returned from the school hall, but only she was at breakfast. As his mother explained, Hal Frobish had left quietly in the early hours to report for his shift on the cipher work, decoding and encoding. It meant they wouldn't be able to attend mass together, but she would go on her own.

What did Rod think of him?

This was a question he was able to answer promptly and frankly. It was obvious that Hal Frobish was a gentleman. He was a treasure, she said: she was more fortunate than she deserved. Once she had completed her instruction and had been received into the Catholic Church, they could marry. And so Rod was more convinced than ever of the degree of change in her. What was it his grandmother had written in her last letter to him? Everyone was capable of turning over a new leaf if the wind was strong enough.

What did Rod intend doing during the day?

Oh, wander around a bit, go for a ferry ride to Manly and back, visit the Domain. He said nothing about calling at the leave and transit depot, nor about clothing coupons.

As he spoke, he became aware that she was staring at him as if broken-hearted about something. A few tears slipped down her cheeks and she dabbed them away.

"It's all my fault," she said.

"What is, Mum?" he asked, deeply concerned.

"You being in the army like you are."

"But I want to be in it."

To this she gave a very positive shake of her head. "No," she said. "I drove you to it. By the way I treated you. Stole your money. How could I ever have done such a terrible thing? No wonder you ran away. There was nowhere else for you to go but into the army. You shouldn't be in uniform. Not at your age."

As he grasped the drift of her concern, Rod grew more and more dismayed.

"It's all my fault," she repeated. "But now you're back home, you're not going up to New Guinea again. You're too young." Rod's dismay turned into horror as she went on. "I talked with Hal about it before he left last night. He said he didn't know the regulations as they operate in the Australian forces, but he'd find out. He said he thought all you'd have to do is tell them you're underage and you'll be automatically discharged."

Or charged with illegally killing the King's enemies, Rod said to himself! By returning to his home territory he had been afraid he was risking being exposed as underage for service, but he could never have foreseen that a major threat would come from his own mother. Not out of mischief or malice, but because she believed that she would be righting a wrong for which she was to blame.

It was with the feeling that he was a fugitive, in enemy territory, that he set out, impelled to do so because of the spell of an exquisite good-night kiss.

12

Quartermaster Sergeant Falbermann was tuning his fiddle at the counter when Rod entered the store, religiously putting in his four hours' practice so that his professional expertise would survive his war service.

"Ah," he said, lowering the instrument but keeping the bow raised. "So you are back with the certificate from the M.O.?"

"No," Rod said. "I'll manage with the boots I've got—until I get back to my unit."

Falbermann chuckled triumphantly. "In other words, you sink better than to try to put it over me, huh. So vy are you here now?"

"I was told I was entitled to clothing coupons."

"Entitled?"

"Yeah."

Falbermann placed his violin and bow on the counter as he prepared for combat.

"Show me your leave pass."

"Why?"

"Because I vill soon tell you to vot or vot not you are entitled."

Rod took out his wallet and extracted the folded leave pass, which he handed to the sergeant, who peered at it hard through his small round spectacles, then started to shake his head and smirk.

"Fife days. That entitles you to nothink. Vun veek you must have at least."

Rod opened up his Record of Service book and showed that he had a credit of forty-one days leave remaining.

"You get nothink for leave you do not take," said the quartermaster, becoming perturbed, because if the young soldier did take all his leave then he would certainly be entitled to coupons.

But Rod had no intention of doing that, especially after discovering his mother's plan for him. So he retrieved his leave pass and returned the documents and wallet to his shirt pocket.

"I'll have to think about it," he told Falbermann.

"You could try the cookhouse."

Was this some sort of obscure joke, Rod asked himself. But he saw that the sergeant was serious.

"Such things as clothing coupons might be available there— for a conzideration."

"Blackmarket, you mean?"

"Who am I to say?" Falbermann said, hunching his shoulders.

"No thanks," said Rod, leaving the quartermaster sergeant unusually perplexed.

Rod walked through the quiet Sunday morning down Oxford Street and by way of the heart of the city to Circular Quay. Young men and women in uniform, posters for enlistment and war bonds, were reminders there was a war on somewhere. Otherwise, here all was easy and carefree and totally unthreatened, an atmosphere which disturbed him when he thought of what would be happening on the New Guinea front, as the newspapers referred to it. He felt as much a deserter from his mates as a fugitive in his home town.

He boarded a Manly ferry, and as it pulled out of Circular Quay he looked across to the gaping giant clown whose open mouth was one of the entrances to Luna Park. He thought of Nugget and how, after they had made up menus of what they would consume when back on leave, they had listed the places they would visit, the fun park opposite high among their choices. Being Sunday, even though it was wintry with gusts of wind and rain showers, dozens of yachts of all sizes were under sail. That the sails should almost all be white did not seem right to Rod. As a token of respect for the sacrifices fellow countrymen were making perhaps there should be black stripes across the sails, in the way that members of bereaved families wore black armbands. Nor did it seem right that the ferries, especially another on the Manly run with smoke blowing forward over its bridge and giving it a beetle-browed look, should still be wearing their red, green, cream, and black livery. Shouldn't they be painted a wartime gray for the duration of the war, like so many of the freighters anchored in the harbor? One of these, after a brush with the enemy at sea, had a hole either side of a forward hold, into which the harbor water freely entered— it seemed to be a slight of some sort when a small hired launch with a cheeky foursome of well-fed Sunday pic- nickers on board puttered in one side of the hold and out the other.

The ferry passengers had music all the way, played by men wearing Great War medal ribbons, a pianist at a fixed position, his upright set near the main middle stairway, a saxophonist, a violinist, and an accordian-player moving between rows of seats as they played, a fifth member of the team following them and rattling coins in a wooden box. Rod dropped in a threepenny piece, mainly because on earlier trips to Manly he had never been able to afford a donation, something which had embarrassed him. Some of the songs were those he had sung at the jungle warfare school and during the unit's rest near Wau: "Roll out the Barrel," "South of the Border," "Ferryboat Serenade," "The Lambeth Walk," and this deepened his sense of having deserted his comrades and his guilt at dallying in such an unthreatened setting.

On the return leg, on a slightly different course, the ferry passed a troop-ship in tropical pale green, almost a cockle-shell compared with the two leviathans he had once seen here. The Harbor Bridge loomed, reminding him of its Opening Day at which he had been present, aged five, up on his father's shoulders, with his mother alongside, before the marriage went sour and the drinking and bickering took over. Nugget, waking from an earlier and milder attack of fever, had claimed he dreamed the bridge had been sliced in two and fallen into the harbor after a secret weapon, a sort of long-range acetylene cutting beam, was aimed at it from the conning tower of a German submarine which had surfaced just off the heads.

After two meat pies, an ice cream, and a bar of chocolate, Rod strolled into the Botanic Gardens, its plots and glades so orderly after the jungle and rain forest that it seemed unreal here, too. A small white butterfly appeared, flying raggedly; it reminded him of Hiroshi Ohara and started him thinking about the picture made from butterfly wings. Rod felt it belonged to Ohara's fiancée, and wondered whether there was any channel through which it might reach her. The International Red Cross, perhaps, which arranged for parcels to be forwarded to prisoners of war and mail sent to relatives. It was too fragile to take back to New Guinea, so he would probably leave it at home. He might even give it to his mother.

In the Domain he recognized a number of regular ranters on boxes, folding steps, and collapsible pulpits, all taking part in a noisy self-indulgence. There were several he believed should be run in by the police, who sauntered about as if deaf to the blasphemy and treason. One black-bearded anarchist wearing a grubby yellow beret claimed that the wars in Europe and the Pacific were engineered by ruthless financial cartels.

For fear he might provoke this man, even by joining his audience, Rod strode away, passing the place where he had once staged a spectacular tumble in the face of jogging soldiers, then roamed around the city, killing time.

Although he had summarily rejected Quartermaster Falbermann's suggestion that he might resort to—or, rather, stoop to—blackmarketeers to obtain clothing coupons, he had in fact given some thought to exploring this avenue. He had no idea how much he would have to pay. But, thinking back on his day so far, the wide-spread self-indulgence and the general indifference he sensed to the struggle going on in the islands up north, even if geographically so remote as to be in another world, persuaded him that he shouldn't have any dealings whatsoever with profiteers. Even to satisfy Brenda, despite the softness of that goodnight kiss and his expectation of others.

As darkness fell he lined up for a free meal at a services canteen near Hyde Park, then crossed to St. Mary's Cathedral and entered a stone version of the moss forest and jungle, with fireflies in the form of burning candles. He sat through the rumble of the rosary and the splendor of benediction, experiencing something of the spell exerted by the rituals of the religion his mother had decided to adopt, savoring the smell of incense, until the celebrating priest, clothed in vestments with a butterfly-like richness of color, raised a brass urn-shaped object to bless the congregation, making the incense-carrying smoke waft out, plunging him back into the moss forest where smoke had been used to screen Ohara's capture—and reminding him of his duplicity.

After walking all the way from the cathedral, it was nearly eight o'clock when he reached Ultimo. He passed the driveway which led to the converted mansion where the Duke-and-Duchess had once lived. He had often thought about that unfortunate man, and only since Dennis Hillyard had revealed something of his own personal dilemma had Rod any glimmering of what might have driven the Duke-and-Duchess to his fate. A few minutes later he knocked on the front door of the Kings' cottage. Alas, the former busy bee, with whose image he had been preoccupied off and on during the day, was in a somewhat stinging mood when she learned that Rod's quest for clothing coupons had been unsuccessful.

"It's a great disappointment," she said, a shapely silhouette in the frame of the open door against a faint gleam of light from within. "I was counting on them."

She implied that because Rod had not obtained the clothing coupons he, too, was due for a disappointment. For all his blind devotion, he could not reveal that by the following Saturday he hoped to be on his way back to New Guinea, and in an attempt to make amends, he took out his wallet and extracted the small folded silk square Ohara had given him. He unfolded it, the cardboard backing lying in the palm of his hand, then tilted it toward her so that it would catch some of the meager luminescence coming from behind her.

"What's it supposed to be?" she asked, a changed note in her voice, struck by its simple beauty.

"New Guinea," Rod told her. "A scene made out of butterfly wings."

"Isn't it pretty!"

"The prisoner I escorted down—he gave it to me."

"But he was a Jap!"

"Of course. He made it."

"That's horrible!"

"Horrible?" Rod was incredulous, for here, as the intelligence major had said, was a thing of true artistry.

"Makes my flesh creep."

"I thought you might like to have it," he said lamely.

"No thank you! They're such monsters!"

"Not all of them."

"How can you say such a thing after what happened on Friday morning." It was obvious Rod knew nothing of what she was referring to. "The hospital ship—they sank it—without warning."

He was confronted with another atrocity, one which complicated and confused his attitude toward the enemy. Well lit up, with red crosses on her sides, the Australian hospital ship *Centaur* had been torpedoed shortly before dawn and had gone down with the loss of doctors, nurses, and crew, all bound for New Guinea to take on more sick and wounded.

The news was still censored but Brenda's mother had heard about it at the officers' club.

He refolded the silk square and slipped it back into his wallet. As he did so, Brenda complained, "I don't understand why you can't get any coupons. All the boys do when they're on leave."

Doubtless "all the boys" had weeks of leave, not just a matter of a few days, long enough to qualify for coupons according to Sergeant Falbermann. Still Rod wasn't prepared to divulge that he was on less than a week's leave, or why.

"Besides," Brenda went on, "I believe they're easily obtainable elsewhere."

"On the blackmarket, you mean? I'm sorry, I can't have anything to do with that sort of thing."

"How ridiculous! Everyone does, in some small way."

"I don't intend to," he said, showing a defiance she had never encountered in him before. And even though it made a strong impression on her, she decided that the evening had to be terminated.

"Please, Rod," she said, "I don't want to argue, not with you of all people. After telling me about that Japanese souvenir, I can understand how Mother felt about the tooth."

"Tooth," said Rod, jarred by its seeming irrelevance.

"The Japanese tooth," Brenda said, as if its part in her mother's life was of such great moment that it merited inclusion in the official history of the war. "An officer staying at the club wanted to give it to her. A tooth with a gold filling, knocked out of the mouth of a dead Japanese general." And with that explained, she put an end to the evening. "I can't ask you in now, I'm too upset. Why don't you come back tomorrow night?"

With this went something more than a mild hint that his

reception could well be dependent upon whether he arrived armed with a peace offering in the form of some clothing coupons.

She closed the door, and he turned away. He sauntered along the footpath as far as the first telegraph pole, then sat down on the curb. At home he expected that his mother would have been talking to Hal Frobish by now about getting him out of the army. If he returned they would probably still be up, and the odds were that they would want to discuss the matter with him. He decided to hang around the streets, then slip home, collect his things, and head through the night to the leave and transit depot, where he would go on parade in the morning.

In the meantime, he felt his feet could do with a proper rest, so he loosened the laces of his boots and hauled them off, placing them either side of him on the footpath, feeling the cool night air caressing his toes through his socks.

Suddenly one of his boots seemed to levitate itself. Glancing up, he saw that it had been lifted by Fran King, who had come outside in a warm dressing-gown and slippers.

Holding the boot horizontally, she moved it forward, then back, and said in a smiling whisper, "You could almost go sailing in it. I could, anyway."

She floated the boot down to where it had been on the footpath, then sat beside him.

"Brenda gets in a real tizz sometimes," she said, peering up into Rod's face, disturbed by his disconsolate expression, anxious to forestall any rift between him and her big sister. "She says things she doesn't really mean. What you want to give her sounds so beautiful."

Realizing she must have overheard him talking to Brenda at the front door, he extracted his wallet and the silk square again, handing it to Fran, leaving her to unfold the material and gasp at what was revealed. The only light out here came from the stars, half of which were clouded over, but simply by its luster the tiny picture revealed something of its magic.

"I'd love to be able to see it in proper light," she said. "Come inside and I'll make some cocoa." As Rod hesitated, she added: "Mum's still at the club. Never gets home till late Sundays."

She carried the butterfly picture very carefully, Rod following her along the narrow side path in his socks, a boot in each hand. Once in the kitchen, she placed the miniature on the table under the electric globe and marveled at the prismatic beauty of the little Garden of Eden.

After she put the kettle on the gas stove, she came back to it and gazed at it again.

"It's like a poem," she said.

Rod scratched his head at the remark. "It could be. I just don't know much about that sort of thing."

"I write poetry sometimes," she told him. "Never show it to anyone, though."

She made the two cups of cocoa. Rod realized he now knew what he should do with the miniature. But first he glanced toward the closed door which led from the kitchen.

Fran said, "If you're worried about Brenda, she's shut herself in her room. We're safe."

"I'd like you to have it," he said, indicating the picture.

"Oh, but I couldn't possibly."

"Why not?"

"It's too precious. Besides, it was given to *you*—and *you* should keep it."

"I can't take it back to the islands, it might get damaged. Please."

"Gee, Rod, I'd treasure it, I really would."

"That's it, then—it's yours."

She wanted to know more about the man who had made it, so Rod told her all he had gleaned about Hiroshi Ohara, how they had met, and what had happened on their journey down to Sydney. She encouraged him to keep talking, and it wasn't long before she knew all about his special friend Nugget Bates, and how Nugget had scared the wits out of him by dreaming that both the *Queen Mary* and the *Queen Elizabeth* had been sunk. And after this, he found himself telling her how he'd made three attempts to join up before he was successful.

"So you put your age on?" she said.

"I had to, didn't I?"

"What about your papers? Who signed them?"

"Do I have to answer that?"

"No—not if you did it yourself."

He grinned and nodded, letting Fran assume he had signed on behalf of his mother, revealing nothing about his grandmother.

"I've been practicing," she said. "And I can imitate Dad's signature perfectly. And Mum's, too, if need be."

"You mean, you're going to have a shot at joining the Women's Land Army?"

"You bet. And I'm getting on, you know—I'll be sixteen in a month's time."

He didn't want to imply any doubt about her chances, but it showed on his face.

"You don't think I can manage it, do you?"

He gave a polite shrug.

"You could be surprised," she told him, standing up, and changing her voice, so that it was slow and deep. "I'm going to borrow a frock and high-heeled shoes from Brenda—and a beret. She won't know about it, of course. I'll do myself up. Plenty of eye-shadow, rouge, lipstick—" As she spoke in this different voice, she went through the actions of applying makeup. "I'll wear earrings, too." With quick twists she screwed on an imaginary pair, first one ear, then the other. "And then," she said, swinging her hips in a slinky walk around the kitchen, "I'll do my hair like this."

Her hair was shoulder-length, and with cupped hands she swept it up either side, revealing the full oval shape of her face as she assumed a sophisticated expression, all of which thoroughly convinced Rod that she could well pass for someone of eighteen, without the aid of a frock, high-heeled shoes, beret, earrings, and makeup.

Laughing at her own impudence, she sat at the kitchen table again to sip her cocoa. Then, growing serious, she said, "You will come back tomorrow night, won't you, Rod?"

He became extremely cagey now, and Fran most concerned.

"Brenda will be hating herself for the way she spoke to you. I know her. And she'll be even more upset if you don't come back. And couldn't you get her some coupons? Just enough for the frock?"

He realized Fran was desperate that what she considered to be a special romance should not be imperiled, so he said, "I'll try."

13

His home cottage was unlit as Rod crept along the side path, then opened the window to his room, with the stealth he had learned after so many jungle patrols, when the mere sound of leaf lightly brushing leaf could alert a hidden enemy. In the darkness of his room he was about to start stuffing his things into his pack, when he suddenly found himself under the full glare of the overhead electric light bulb. Hal Frobish stood in pajamas beside the wall switch, a glass of water in one hand. He put a finger to his lips and closed the bedroom door very gently behind him.

"I was getting myself a drink," he whispered. "Saw your shadow passing the kitchen window." He pointed to the pack in Rod's hands. "If you're planning on leaving, forget it. Maybe you are underage for army service, but your mother won't be doing anything about it. I spoke with her last night and told her I figured all she would do is break your heart. You want to get back up there with your pals, don't you?"

" 'Course I do," said Rod in a thick whisper.

"Your mother sees my point. She won't be standing in your way."

"Thanks," Rod said awkwardly.

"Try to spend a few days with her before you head off."

Rod said he would do his best, and Frobish returned to sleep for a few hours before leaving to go on his next cipher shift. Rod slept until after he had gone. He expected his mother also to have left, as he had gathered she started at seven-thirty at the war clothing factory, but she was waiting to make him breakfast. He was worried that she might be suffering from something of her old Mondayitis again, not going to work after the weekend.

"I'm entitled to time off," she explained. "Especially when you're home on leave. Hal's going to phone the head inspector for me. It'll be all right. What are you going to do today?"

He very nearly said: "Hide!" Perhaps he didn't need to go to that extreme, although, after the run-in with that former rival at the dance, he felt it could be dangerous for him to be seen locally. On the other hand, he should call at the leave and transit depot and start making inquiries about getting back to his unit.

The radio news made him all the more anxious to be on his way. As he ate a large breakfast of his favorite dish of fried bread, bacon, eggs, tomatoes, and chips, and a stack of toast, he heard a summary of what had been happening in New Guinea. Australian and American positions had been dive-bombed and strafed, while allied patrols had been active in the Mubo area. So the stronghold had not yet fallen.

His mother made just one reference to what she had discussed with Frobish. "I still feel it's wrong for you to go back, but it's your decision. I'm not too sure, but probably Hal was right to persuade me to change my mind."

Rod resigned himself to having to lie low in the house all day. He listened to the radio, hearing serials which seemed to have been running, with much the same voices, ever since he could remember. But the news bulletins made him desperate to do something about getting back to the mountain ranges and ridges.

In the end, he told his mother that he was going out to see some more of his home town, but in fact he headed by the shortest route to the leave and transit depot.

He didn't expect a priority air passage, but was depressed at what he discovered. All the trains going north were heavily booked by reinforcements and other units; and because of subs lurking along the coast, few drafts were going by ship. The transit sergeant advised him, "Take some more leave."

But he had taken five days, and the three days he'd nearly had—Saturday, Sunday, and so far on Monday—were proving more than enough. If he checked back in he could go on parade every morning.

"You can do that until you're blue in the face," the transit sergeant told him, "but it probably won't get you anywhere."

Rod decided to leave his decision until the next day.

Concerned as he was with the war bulletins, he had been thinking about Brenda as well. He felt that he couldn't leave for the islands again without being on good terms with her, and the answer to this was not far away. So doing what many a male had done before him, he rationalized the situation and decided to at least investigate the possibility of obtaining some clothing coupons. At the back of the depot cookhouse, he found a grubby duty cook smoking an

American cigar as he sat in a deck chair, reading the racing news.

Noting Rod's presence simply by seeing his boots, but not raising his eyes, apparently unimpressed by their size and therefore having no particular interest in seeing what their owner looked like, the cook asked, "Whadda ya want, sport?"

"I was wondering . . ." Rod began.

"Cigarettes, biscuits, tinned fruit?" And when Rod didn't respond, he looked up at last. "What is it, then?"

"Clothing coupons."

"How many?"

"Well, at least thirteen," Rod said, remembering the number Brenda had told him were required for a frock.

The cook shook his head. "Fifty at least."

Rod was prepared to be confronted with an impossible price for the minimum order, but before he could ask what it was, the cook gave it to him.

"Five quid."

"For fifty?"

"Make it four."

"Four pounds?" Rod said, making sure he had the price right.

"Take it or leave it."

"No, no. I'll have them."

The cook tugged up his apron and dug into his trousers for a bulging wallet. Rod had drawn his ten pounds leave money in single one pound and ten shillings notes; he quickly counted out the required sum, and in return was given the fifty coupons.

His mother had promised him a roast lamb dinner, and he had told her he would be home for it. Hal Frobish wouldn't be there; his shift didn't end until midnight. Back home, the radio was on again, another serial, but with some action in contrast to the sob stuff he'd heard that morning.

Now that he had the clothing coupons in his possession, he couldn't help but look forward to presenting them to Brenda. Having done this, he would then feel he could go back to the islands, his relationship with her under no cloud. He would have kept faith with Fran, too.

He hoed into a huge plate of roast lamb and trimmings—until the seven o'clock news came on, starting with the latest from the New Guinea front. The combined Australian and American forces in the Wau, Bobdubi, and Mubo areas had come under ferocious attack, up to forty bombers at a time and packs of low-flying fighters strafing lines of communication, threatening to cut off front-line infantry and commando units which had also suffered casualties from Japanese ground forces. The Mubo area had taken the full brunt of the attacks.

Rod dropped his knife and fork. His food threatened to choke him.

His mother was alarmed as he stood up, saying, "I'm sorry, Mum—that's it. I've gotta go."

"But where?"

"To the leave and transit depot—to try to get back up there. My unit's in the thick of it."

"Oh Rod, you can't leave without at least finishing your dinner."

So he had to force himself to eat while the news reader continued. The summary repeated the New Guinea dispatches, and this time he headed straight for his room, stuffed his gear into his pack, put on his great coat, slipped on the shoulder straps of the pack and returned to the sitting room, where his mother had been crying.

"I'm sorry, Mum," he repeated. "I've just gotta go."

He had something to give her, the fifty clothing coupons.

"You can probably make some use of these," he said. "Say cheerio to Hal for me. If anyone wants to know why I had to leave so soon, maybe tell them I got urgent orders to report back."

Though quite tall herself, his mother still had to reach up to embrace him. He responded by putting his arms around her, and they clung to each other, the years falling away, becoming truly mother and son again, as they had been when she used to cuddle him when he was small and tell him how much she treasured him. How would she be able to get in touch with him? He trusted her now, so wrote down his number and unit—and revealed that he had enlisted under her maiden name, McKenzie.

Since it was the quickest way to get there, he walked to the showgrounds, aware that his boots were giving his feet some nips and twinges again.

Every morning for the next week, Rod appeared on the first parade, only to be told to turn out again next day and draw a twenty-four hours leave pass if he wanted to. Then his name was called, but he found himself detailed to an infantry battalion stationed in the Northern Territory, and it was only after some heavy pleading with a warrant officer that his name was removed from the draft. And so he was back again on the daily parade of hopefuls, which, of course, included non-hopefuls, only too happy to have their Sydney stays extended.

During this week, the sinking of the hospital ship *Centaur* was officially announced. On the other side of the world, RAF bombers had breached the Mohne Dam in the Ruhr. In New Guinea, Japanese bombers were still attacking Australian positions and their fighters strafing the supply lines north from Wau to Mubo.

He tracked down Horrie one night, noting that at least the war hadn't changed the night sky, and that you didn't have to look long before you could see the brief glowing plume of a falling star.

"Jeez," the milk carter said. "We all thought you'd gone."

"Could be any day now," Rod said.

"Hey, remember that actress—the gum-boot chucker?"

How could Rod ever forget?

"I was tellin' her you'd been back. She wanted to know whether you'd found out what it was all about yet?"

Grinning wryly, Rod said, "What'd you say?"

"I dunno if you've cracked it yet, do I? But I reckon you coulda done all right with them King sisters if you'd stayed around."

Rod revealed nothing. He could easily go over to Ultimo, but he had made his partings, and he was glad he no longer possessed temptation in the form of clothing coupons.

Meanwhile, he had discovered why his feet were sore. It wasn't so much the boots being too small as the condition of his feet. Chilblains were making them swell. As soon as he moved north to the warmth, that problem would be solved—but he would still need new, larger boots.

It was after a few more days, when he realized he had been three whole weeks in Sydney, that he thought of a way of trying to escape from the clutches of the leave and transit depot. The intelligence officer, Major Pender, had expressly told him to call should he need help. So he went to Victoria Barracks and faced up to a suspicious adjutant, who cross-questioned him before revealing that the major was away at a staff school and would be there for another month. Could anyone else help? Perhaps Private Iris, whose surname he didn't know? He was told she was taking her leave while her boss was away—and in any case, what the devil did he think *she* might be able to do!

And so all Rod succeeded in doing was getting a brush-off. He pottered around the city until he reckoned Horrie would have started his deliveries. Just for something to do, if Horrie needed a hand, Rod was willing to help.

"Been hoping you'd turn up," said Horrie. He dug into a knee pocket of his khaki overalls and brought out a letter. "Been carrying this around for a coupla nights."

It was from Nugget Bates, addressed to Horrie, with a note for him and a letter to Rod. Nugget said that he was fit and well again; in fact "the stupid bastard of an M.O. had no right to send me to the hospital as I was over the worst of the fever." He nearly hadn't survived being taken there, because "the bloody stretcher-bearers slipped crossing a fast jungle stream and I was nearly brained by the rocks and drowned at the same time." Finally, Rod would be pleased to know that one pair of new boots for him had been delivered, and that Nugget was "shaking the centipedes and scorpions out of them every morning."

With this problem solved, Rod became more optimistic. Three days later he was allotted a seat on a troop train as far as another leave and transit depot, the one in the Brisbane showgrounds. Here he had to spend a full week before heading farther north on one of the world's slowest trains, which took five days to get to Townsville, due to long waits in sidings. Trains with whole fighting units bypassed them going north, and trains loaded with vital minerals headed south.

From Townsville it was either by plane or ship across the Coral Sea to Port Moresby, but at the leave and transit depot here he faced the same situation. He started taking twenty-four hour leave passes again, spending a few hours each night in the canteens and clubs, then going on parade next morning. He had no desire for another sea voyage now, but hoped to fly.

A different problem had loomed. He'd had a supply of atebrin pills when he left his unit, but they had run out—and the medical orderly at the depot couldn't supply him with any more. They could only be issued once he was in New Guinea. If the parasites from the malaria-carrying mosquito were in his system, after a few weeks without the shield of the atebrin, he could go down with the fever—and that meant a spell in the hospital. So every time he shivered—and the Townsville nights could be sharp at this time of the year—he feared the worse.

After being unsuccessful for the third morning in a row, a transit officer called him over once the parade had been dismissed.

Rod's first reaction was that the truth about his real age had caught up with him, and that, after battling his way this far up the coast, he was about to have his army career terminated.

The officer, a captain, eyed the color-patch on the faded puggaree band on Rod's slouch hat, then asked for the lance corporal's name, number, and unit.

Standing at attention, Rod gave the particulars, as if they were part of the description of a condemned man; but to his astonishment the officer's attitude underwent a remarkable change.

"So you're Lance Corporal Rodney McKenzie?"

"That's right, sir."

"Stand easy." And as Rod responded, the captain put out his hand and Rod's was treated to a crushing shake as the officer went on, "My heartiest congratulations, McKenzie.

A list of decorations has just been promulgated. You've been awarded the Military Medal."

The transit officer escorted Rod to his office where he read out the citation. The award was for signal bravery in helping in the capture of a valuable Japanese prisoner. The captain called in a staff-sergeant and instructed him to go to the QM Store and obtain some of the red, white, and blue ribbon, and a mount, for the hero.

"Now," said the captain, approaching Rod's most pressing problem. "A man like you deserves some sort of priority to get back to his unit. I'll see what can be done."

Next day, Rod handed in his heavy trousers and great coat at the QM Store; then, wearing his medal ribbon on his shirt just above the left-hand pocket, he was put on a plane to Port Moresby with a priority connection to Wau. Thus, after five weeks and a final trudge in boots which were giving him what was unmistakably final notice that they could no longer accommodate his feet, he reached his unit—and a new pair of made-to-measure brown army boots.

Part
Three

14

In the time Rod had been away, his unit had crept, clawed, burrowed, and blasted its way closer to the Japanese stronghold at Mubo.

Back in the heat and humidity, and after splashing and squelching from Wau through water and mud, in between hitching rides on jeeps and trucks, Rod's feet had become unbearably swollen. The unit's position was again on the lee slope of a ridge, the main shelters still tent-flys on untrimmed lengths of local timber. As well as keeping Rod's new boots free of lethal insects, Nugget had applied waterproofing. Before Rod could try them on, he had to remove those he was wearing—and it required help from his mate to pull them off. And then, as Rod gave his feet an airing, Nugget conducted an eager interrogation, wasting little time in bringing up the subject of the two King sisters, something that had in fact occupied Rod's thoughts ever since having left home in Ultimo. He could not forget Brenda and that goodnight kiss. Nor Fran's exhilarating sparkle and transformation when she swept up her hair.

He admitted to having seen them but that, despite Nugget's persistence, was all. Besides, he wanted to be brought up to date in what had happened in his absence, and as he pulled on a fresh pair of socks and sampled the roomy luxury of the new made-to-measure boots which, like their predecessors, would become almost part of his body, he learned that while the unit had made advances, it had not done so without having to give ground at times; and that while it had ambushed enemy patrols, its own patrols had been ambushed. Its strength was down because of the sick, the wounded, and the dead; Lieutenant Paine had been killed by a shell from a Japanese mountain gun, but the platoon was otherwise intact. As for his own section, Privates Larry Donald and Fred Mullen were still, to use an expression from the Great War, swinging the lead (even if the metal involved was gold) and had been using dubious ailments to keep themselves on light duties.

Nugget couldn't have been more pleased with his mate's Military Medal if he had won it himself. He insisted Rod must keep wearing the ribbon. After all, what was good enough for an officer was good enough for a member of the other ranks, and their company commander always wore the ribbon of his Military Cross. Rod could take only a limited pride in the award; he still felt he had obtained it at the expense of betraying Hiroshi Ohara, and that he wasn't really entitled to a decoration when he had been away, leaving his mates to do the fighting. And so, when the new platoon commander, the former Sergeant Pollock, called for two volunteers to go on an information-gathering raid, it was a chance to make amends, and Rod promptly stepped forward.

Not on his own. Nugget followed—almost a pace and a

half to his mate's one to stand alongside him. Nugget's curiosity about the King girls played a part in his decision; he knew Rod well enough to suspect that his reticence on the subject could mean there was something to be revealed. Away together, Rod might be in a better frame of mind to confide.

Rod would have liked to have felt able to confide, but on another matter: his new ambivalent attitude toward the Japanese. He didn't need to question Nugget to know that there had been no change in *his* attitude: the Jap remained a fanatical beast to be hunted down and destroyed. Thus Rod was fearful of giving Nugget any inkling of how his contact with the prisoner Ohara had affected him, even in the face of the sinking of the hospital ship.

However, Rod's feelings toward the enemy were soon to undergo a further complication, while Nugget's hopes of being alone with his mate were put to an end by what Captain Exton had to tell them.

"It's all very well for intelligence to keep complaining that we're not supplying them with enough information, they don't seem to realize how hard it is to come by. So we've suggested that Lieutenant Hillyard go along with you. It should help to have someone who knows Japanese."

Showing open dismay, Rod and Nugget looked at each other; but Exton had something to add. "You'll be in charge at all times, McKenzie. Hillyard will obey your commands even though he may be a commissioned officer."

"Pity you haven't got a blackboard and chalk," Nugget said, when Exton had finished briefing them and they had moved away from his tent. "You could give him a few lines to write."

"I wouldn't know what to set him," said Rod, grinning.

"I'll tell you what. 'Don't Bugger About'!"

"Don't get it," Rod said.

"There's a story going round that Prickle-head was caught in the act with a joker from signals—and that they're both going to be charged."

From the haunted appearance of Hillyard when he arrived later in the morning, Rod could well believe that what Nugget had told him was true.

"Congratulations on your Military Medal," he said. "I trust you enjoyed your leave."

"Thanks," Rod replied in answer to the congratulations; and then, referring to the leave, he said, "I didn't really."

"Anxious to be back here to help win the war, eh?"

Hillyard's flair for sarcasm had not deserted him, even though he might be in grave trouble.

Their objective was a nest of huts in a fortified compound. They had been located by a spotter plane after being erected by natives who still sided with the Japanese, a sign that the indigenous inhabitants thought the invaders from the north might emerge as victors.

The trail they were to take, a circuitous one to give them as much cover as possible, would bring them to the perimeter of the Japanese position in about ten minutes. An air strike had been arranged with the Americans to hit at the far side of the position, but to leave the huts intact.

Before the three raiders set out, Nugget quietly enjoyed the situation, especially when Rod handed Hillyard a tin of dark-green blacking and told him to smear some of it on his face. The schoolmaster obeyed with marked lack of enthusiasm. They left the camp with Rod in the lead, carrying his rifle; then Hillyard, followed by Nugget, both with Owen submachine guns.

As jungle walks went it was one which Rod could be said to have enjoyed; his new, comfortable boots seemed to make him capable of much greater stealth—and he had to exercise more of this than the other two, since he was so much bigger and therefore in greater danger of becoming entangled with growths along the sides of the tunnel trail and overhead.

The immediate approaches to the Japanese position looked harmless enough, but Rod carefully lifted some of the jungle debris, to show Hillyard long strips of bamboo which would give out loud crackling sounds if anyone stepped on them.

The three waited for the dive-bombers on the edge of the trap, among bushes with umbrella-sized leaves. The planes arrived right on time, four of them, with an escort of two fighters. As the bombers unleashed their loads on the far side of the Japanese position, the jungle reverberated to the detonations, which drowned out the cracklings of the concealed bamboo strips as Rod raced across them, leading Hillyard and Nugget—only to run into another warning device: barbed wire lightly hidden by creepers and strung with empty ration tins which clanked and clattered as they bounced against one another. But the booming echoes from the surrounding valleys and ridges masked the noise.

Little could be seen overhead, until, through a gap in the jungle canopy, they glimpsed an American Lightning being chased by a Japanese Zero, which had apparently coincided an aerial reconnaissance with the bombing. The dive-bombers and the other escorting fighter withdrew, leaving the remaining Lightning and the Zero to scream and whine, their machine guns rattling and stuttering. They swept so low that spent cartridge cases showered on the trees and acrid cordite and engine fumes made the eyes of the three raiders smart and water, and forced them to suppress choking coughs before they could continue forward.

While the dog-fight continued, the Lightning on the Zero's tail, then the Zero on the swallow-like tail of the Lightning, the raiders reached the edge of the Japanese compound at a point not far from the huts. They crouched, one knee on the ground, behind screens of large-leafed jungle growths. Sentries had their backs to them, all looking up at the aerial duel. Other members of the garrison were beside bunkers and foxholes, some still in slit trenches. A Japanese officer, a captain, stood in the doorway of what appeared to be the main hut; then, one hand on the hilt of a heavy sword, he swaggered out into the open for a better view of the twists, figures of eight, and other desperate contortions as first one fighter gained the ascendency, then the other.

Rod decided the hut from which the Japanese captain had emerged was his target; he signaled Hillyard and Nugget, and they worked their way around within the undergrowth bordering the compound until they were opposite the rear of the hut, which had a low-silled open window. From this point Rod would make a dash for the hut, slip inside and grab whatever he could in the way of documents. Crouching as before, he waited to pick his time.

The duel ended suddenly. A burst from the Zero started a fire in the Lightning, which went into a steep dive, flame and smoke streaming from one of its engine pods. The pilot appeared to tumble out of the cockpit; a tiny white umbrella jerked open, then the main parachute blossomed, and the khaki-clad pilot swung wildly. His plane vanished from sight to crash moments later, creating another series of violent echoes. As lurid smoke began to rise, the pilot controlled his descent, pulling on the ropes of his parachute to try to bring himself down in a hole in the jungle below; but as he did so, he became a target for ground fire, one Japanese marksman in a slit trench opening up on him, others joining in—until all were stopped and silenced by an angry shout from the captain.

Rod whispered to Hillyard, "What's he saying?"

So far the schoolmaster had been a model of a well-disciplined jungle fighter. Now Hillyard failed to answer, and before Rod could repeat the question, the Zero buzzed the compound, the pilot waving to those below, before corkscrewing in a victory roll as he turned east toward his base in New Britain.

Rod whispered again. "What did he say?"

Hillyard's mouth hung open and no words came, and before Rod realized that he was dumb with fear, he added, "Come on—you're supposed to know Japanese."

But Hillyard still couldn't get anything out, and the same thought came to both his companions: instead of being of help to them, the intelligence officer was turning into an encumbrance.

Finally Hillyard managed to whisper that the Japanese officer wanted the pilot to be taken prisoner and brought to the compound. Then, gaining better control of himself, Hillyard went on, "This must be Captain Astashi—he fits the description the captured butterfly hunter gave of his O.C. A tyrant."

The captain appeared to live up to his reputation, his swagger becoming more pronounced, one hand remaining on the hilt of his sword as he moved across the compound to where the captured flyer would be brought, assuming he survived the parachute descent. Other Japanese in the compound, including sentries, kept looking in the same direction, as Rod soon observed. This was his chance; he decided to seize it. He whispered to Nugget and Hillyard to cover him as best they could, but if things went wrong to get out of the place quick.

He chose a gap between the leaves so that he would not create a rustle as he left their protection. Then, at a crouching run he reached the rear of Captain Astashi's hut, and, in a continuous movement, stepped over the low sill of the open window into a sparsely-furnished interior, where he glimpsed a small movable shrine, but more importantly a folding desk on which were letters, maps, other documents, and what was either a manual or a code book, all of which he swiftly stuffed inside his shirt in the manner of a famished beggar loose in a food store. Then, stepping out the way he had entered, he checked around, saw only Japanese backs facing him, so made a stooped dash back to his previous cover, going down again on one knee beside Nugget and Hillyard. All of which he completed not a moment too soon: Astashi glanced around and noted two sentries more interested in the anticipated arrival of the captured pilot than in patrolling the compound. He screamed at them to attend to their duties, and so a sentry began to pace up and down along the perimeter, passing within a few yards of the three raiders. Rod was confident that he had made a substantial haul, but there was no knowing how long they might have to remain here. Not to head back the way they'd come in could involve unknown hazards.

The waiting also seemed an ordeal for Captain Astashi. He walked on his heels and kept stamping about, several times on the verge of going back into his hut, in which case Rod expected another sort of explosion the moment he discovered what was missing from his desk. But then, preceded by a chattering hullabaloo, the young American pilot was escorted into the compound, his hands tied in front by rope cut from the cords of his parachute, which two Japanese soldiers carried, while others bore pieces of his clothing, right down to his flying boots and underpants; he was using his tied hands to cover his genitals. By denuding him thus, to increase his sense of shame for daring to take part in an attack on the sons of their illustrious Emperor, the Japanese revealed him for what he was—a superb example of young Caucasian manhood, aged about twenty-two, his fair skin, blond hair, and searingly blue eyes suggesting Scandinavian ancestry. As he was brought to a halt in front of Astashi, he displayed no fear, keeping his strong chin uplifted in defiance.

Astashi began a hysterical harangue, accompanied by much fist-shaking; then he drew his sword out of its ornamental scabbard and started waving it wildly. Obviously he was making threats, and Rod and Nugget looked to Hillyard to interpret them.

"He keeps harking back to General Doolittle's raid on Tokyo last year," Hillyard whispered, referring to the daring American sortie made by planes from an aircraft carrier. "Some of his relatives were killed, he claims; he plans to exact retribution on their behalf."

The horrifying nature of the vengeance became apparent when the captive's arms were pinioned with more cord cut from his parachute and some of its silk used to bind his eyes. He was led to the end of a slit trench where he was forced to kneel and lower his head, jabs of sharp-tipped bayonets prodding him to make him obey, drawing trickles of blood from his back and buttocks.

In his role of executioner, Captain Astashi wiped the blade of his sword with a white silk scarf. After lightly touching the back of the American pilot's neck with its razor edge, he lifted it in readiness to bring it down.

Hillyard was so agitated that he squirmed convulsively. "We must do something," he said, dangerously above a whisper.

"There's nothing we can do," Rod told him. "Unless we want to be mown down. Our first duty is to get the captured stuff back to the unit. You should know that."

"We can't allow this to happen," Hillyard pleaded.

"Listen, mate," Nugget said. "Shut up or we'll all be copping it."

The sword flashed down, severing the young man's head, which plummetted into the trench. A kick from Astashi and his torso, from which blood spurted, toppled after it.

Hillyard vomited to one side, a sound lost in the jubilant shouts from most, but not all, of Astashi's men. The captain wiped the blade of his sword with the silk scarf, then slid it back into its scabbard. After another order, which Hillyard was in no condition to interpret, but which Rod and Nugget presently understood, two of his troops came forward with shovels and started to fill in the slit trench.

Rod, too, felt like throwing up—and as if to remind him of the dilemma into which this latest act of brutality by the Japanese had landed him, a blue-green butterfly fluttered around in the compound over the site where the young pilot was being buried.

Then Hillyard began to mutter in English and Japanese, calling Astashi a barbarian in both languages.

Rod held up a hand at him for silence. "When they find what's missing from the hut, they'll go berserk," he whispered. "It might give us a chance to make a run for it."

They waited for Captain Astashi to swagger back to his

hut, but before he did so, something which had already accounted for the deaths of members of this very Japanese unit, was spotted by a sentry. Giant bootprints between the edge of the undergrowth surrounding the compound and the captain's hut. He cried out in alarm, pointing to his find, as the captain and other soldiers came running.

"Mate, we're gone now," Nugget groaned.

But it was Hillyard who decided their fates were not inevitably sealed. He rose to his feet, saying, "You two make a run for it." And before Rod could ask him what the hell he thought he was playing at, Hillyard surged forward out of the undergrowth and into the compound, shouting in English and Japanese, accusing Astashi of the ultimate in barbarity by wantonly slaying a beautiful human being in full flower of his manhood. At the same time he opened up with his submachine gun. Rod and Nugget glimpsed Astashi throwing himself to the ground, and sentries opening up at the interloper; then they turned about and hurtled through the undergrowth, across the concealed barbed wire and bamboo strips, the noise of the dancing tins and the cracklings this time drowned out by submachine-gun fire from the compound. As they reached the track, the fire petered out and was replaced by baying sounds as vengeful Japanese started to pursue them. But they had sufficient start to reach the point where men from another platoon were waiting to cover their return.

"You've got a whopper of a haul here," Captain Exton told Rod, after he had finished emptying the front of his shirt. "Lieutenant Hillyard's intelligence colleagues won't be able to complain about this lot."

With platoon commander Pollock, Exton examined some

of the documents, several of which seemed to confirm that fresh Japanese reinforcements were still slipping in. Before contacting headquarters, Exton looked Rod in the eye, then Nugget, and asked, "Why do you reckon Hillyard took it into his head to do what he did?"

Nugget had already put this very question to Rod when they had reached the waiting troops.

Rod had answered, "If that pilot had been a blonde, what would you have done?"

"A girl, y'mean?"

"Yeah. Would you have held back from having a go?"

It was beyond Nugget to consider that any measure of tolerance might be shown toward the feelings of a homosexual, so he flatly rejected the notion. "What would a blonde be doin' parachutin' out of a fighter plane?"

Rod left it at that.

Now, in front of their company commander, Nugget looked to Rod for a lead; and when Rod shrugged, Nugget shrugged too.

"As you may or may not have heard," Exton went on, "Lieutenant Hillyard was, how shall I put it, in a spot of bother. It didn't strike either of you as being, shall we say, some sort of an equivalent act to hara-kiri?"

The two mates answered with a further shrug apiece; while Rod, who again was marginally the first to decide, recalled his grandmother saying: "A blind eye's a very handy thing to have in this life, Rodney—never be afraid to use it."

And so Rod said, "If Lieutenant Hillyard hadn't drawn the Japanese fire, we wouldn't be back here now."

"That decides it, then," Exton said.

The impending charge against the former schoolmaster and that against the signals private were forgotten; Hillyard was awarded a posthumous Military Cross for exceptional bravery in action.

The threat that his presence had always posed to Rod, that his true age might be revealed, was removed. But he still had Privates Larry Donald and Fred Mullen to contend with. And his promotion just then to full corporal didn't help him.

15

As they rested under their tent-fly after the raid, with mugs of coffee brought up from the cookhouse, Nugget at last managed to start Rod talking about what had happened after he had been hustled south. While Rod still gave no hint of any change in his attitude toward the Japanese race, Nugget seemed satisfied that he had extracted a comprehensive report from his mate, though Rod himself felt there was something he was holding back, undefined even to himself, to do with Brenda and Fran.

Concerning Larry Donald and Fred Mullen, Rod learned from Nugget that it was generally assumed the pair had a secret setup in an abandoned camp back toward Wau. Rod guessed they would have been trying to devise some way of transferring their hoard of gold to the Australian mainland; he had no doubt that when they were on light duties they were in fact hard at work in their own interests.

He realized he must try to pull them into line, but put it off for a few days in the aftermath of the raid. Being forced to witness the execution of the young American pilot had left Rod in a state of shock. Nugget, too. It had been made so much worse for them by not being free to intervene. And coming as it did after the sinking of the hospital ship, it unsettled Rod's conclusions about the true nature of the Japanese. One thing it did not shake was his belief that the war in the Pacific, like its counterpart in Europe, was unquestionably against the forces of evil. Of this he was more certain than ever, making it all the more important to him that he should see the conflict through—especially the current campaign, which would not end with the fall of Mubo, but only when the way was clear to the capture of the base farther north at Salamaua.

Each section of the platoon must try to operate at full strength; Rod could not have men in his section on light duties, or worse still, malingering. He bearded Donald and Mullen outside their tent-fly and told them he expected them to do their fair share of soldiering in the push to come. Each brazenly wore a lump of solid gold in the form of a signet ring, like part of a knuckle-duster.

"Listen, kid," Mullen said, "I've done my fair share an' more. This is my second world war."

"Yes," said Rod, going on to repeat what he had heard often enough to know it by heart. "Gallipoli was nothing like the Somme—and the Somme was nothing like this."

"Smart aleck, eh," Donald said.

"No," Rod answered evenly. "I believe Fred." In fact, he had heard Mullen turn the statement around and claim that New Guinea had nothing on the conditions on the Somme.

"There's somethin' else you'd better believe," Donald told Rod. "Instead of that medal ribbon, you'll be wearin' rompers if it gets out how old you really are. So do yourself a favor and bugger off."

"You should be put on a charge for that," Rod said, still keeping his cool.

"Of course I should—but you won't be doin' it."

"There could come a time."

"Not as long as your real name's 'Murray.' "

Donald gave a malicious laugh as he saw the concern flicker in the lance corporal's eyes.

"All right," Rod said, "you might as well tell me what you know."

"The facts. Got 'em from the late Lieutenant Poofter Hillyard."

So before ending up a hero, the schoolmaster had reneged on the pact he had made with his former pupil. Not that it surprised Rod all that much. His grandmother had once warned him: "You can count the people you can trust on the fingers of one hand, especially if it's cut off at the wrist." But it hadn't really been a betrayal.

"I got an inklin' when you met up with Hillyard back at Wau. He called you 'Murray' first up, didn't he?"

Rod hadn't realized that Donald had picked this up and remembered it.

"Got talkin' to him when you was back on the mainland. Checked out with him when you was at his school. Did some sums, an' came up with your age. You're still way underage." And then Rod's size somehow became a menace and Donald did a quick switch, giving an easy laugh and going on to say, "Only pullin' your leg, of course—you know that."

"Pull my leg if you like," Rod said. "As long as you pull your weight."

Thus Rod was stuck with the same sort of compromise he had been forced to come to with Hillyard.

Two weeks later, Mubo fell. The documents filched in the raid on Captain Astashi's hut played no small part. Once it was discovered that reinforcements were being smuggled into the stronghold and where they were landing and the tracks they were taking, countermeasures put an end to that inflow. Intense fighting followed, attack and counter-attack, with losses on both sides, although those of the enemy were higher, almost a thousand dead. The Japanese began to withdraw farther north to positions nearer Salamaua, and as they did so there were signs that they were vacating the Mubo stronghold. Natives who had been working with them appeared at Australian and American positions, swearing on mildewed mission Bibles that they had cooperated with the Japanese only because they had been threatened with reprisals if they did not conform.

Rod's unit began to gird itself for what was expected to be the final round of the campaign, although the battle was still against not only a human or sub-human enemy, but also the weather and the terrain. They were in high country now, often with cloud in teased-out layers below them. In damp and drizzle they lived with misty ghosts, scraps of cloud which hovered or drifted, ever threatening to turn into something more substantial, hostile soldiers, so that nerves were constantly on edge, even those of the most sanguine of men, the most fearless. Because of intelligence warnings that the Japanese might use gas, they all had respirators, although they did not carry this equipment, except for the plastic gas capes, which gave better protection against the weeping atmosphere and torrential downpours than ground sheets.

Rampant funguses made no distinction between friend and foe. Swiftly-spreading warts grew on the living; toadstools in small brown and purple crops on the unburied dead. Victims of skin eruptions lined up to be treated by the M.O. or his orderly with violet, green, and yellow antiseptic dyes, making them look as if their skins had been colorfully patched.

Before Mubo fell, Nugget had been aware that Rod had not written a single letter, even though Nugget had suggested he should at least let his mother and Horrie Benson know that he had been awarded the Military Medal. Nugget himself had used a pile of Red Shield Salvation Army notepaper to keep in touch with members of his vast family and his friends.

In this period, Rod received two letters, neither of which mentioned his decoration, one from his mother just to let him know that she and Hal were well. The other was from Horrie, beginning with his usual cheery "Good day mate." He was still surviving, even though he was due to have another mouth to feed, as his wife was expecting again "which says something for a man who is hardly ever home at night"; "a couple of pie-eyed Yanks" had tried to commandeer Edgar and the milk cart, but "the noble nag" had dug in his hooves and refused to move; two Elizabeth Bay society matrons had crept out in their dressing-gowns with buckets and trowels to collect Edgar's droppings because of the shortage of fertilizer for their roses and had "staged a private war over a great dollop of steaming manure." Finally, he said that young Fran King was no longer tending the horses at the depot, as she had somehow managed to con her way into the Women's Land Army. Rod pictured her in uniform, laughing.

Some two weeks after the fall of Mubo, shortly before Rod's seventeenth birthday, what the postal orderly described as a poultice of mail arrived. Nugget received his usual wad, but he seemed to be more interested in the two letters addressed to "Full" Corporal Rodney McKenzie M.M., one of normal size in his mother's handwriting, the other an unusually fat one from Horrie.

It didn't take Rod long to discover what had happened, and Nugget was waiting with a mischievous grin for his reactions, since he had taken it upon himself to write to two addresses in Ultimo.

"I oughta brain you!" Rod said, as Nugget's laughter gurgled up.

His mother was ecstatic. Perhaps he remembered his grandmother telling them that some of their ancestors had won medals in their day. Hal Frobish also sent his congratulations on the second stripe.

Horrie's note was short, offering Rod "congrats on the gong" and enclosing two unaddressed envelopes from "female fans." The one Rod read first was from Brenda, because he recognized her writing, a precise girlish hand which hadn't matured much since he had helped her with her homework. It was rather formal in tone. Brenda seemed most concerned to let him know that "mother sends her warmest congratulations on your brave deed." It was almost as if the letter had been dictated by Helen King, although at its end he found something of the lingering softness of her goodnight kiss when she wrote "Fondest best wishes."

Fran's letter was lively, dashed off in high spirits. She had two days' leave from looking after pigs and poultry with her Women's Land Army unit, and was at home when Horrie called in to break the wonderful news. "Brenda's wildly excited about it and has been telling all her friends," she wrote. The Land Army was great fun, even if "at times it is a bit hard to keep looking the part, if you know what I mean." She ended with "Lots of Love."

To satisfy Nugget's curiosity, he handed his mate both

letters, although without a page that had been enclosed with Fran's. Nugget wanted to know what Fran was hinting at when she wrote that it was hard to keep looking the part, so Rod told him how she had planned to get into the Land Army by making herself look older.

"She sure sounds fun," Nugget said.

Rod had already been thinking the very same thing, especially after having read the enclosed single-page poem. Something which had been lurking in his mind had now asserted itself, and it dismayed him when Nugget went on, "How would it be, if when we get back—if ever, that is—I looked her up? You wouldn't mind, would you?"

"Why should I?" Rod managed to say, without revealing any of his concern. A dogged loyalty to Brenda had been blinding him to what was happening. He had been lingering over thoughts about Fran, right back to her offer to partner him at the school dance after Brenda had given him up as a hopeless case. From every meeting with her since, he had retained something to remember. Brenda was fated to become more and more like her mother. Fran had been gradually replacing her in his mind, in the same sort of way that his obsession with big ships had been partly superseded by his infatuation with Brenda, before his dedication to his role as a soldier became dominant. It was Fran's poem that finally opened his eyes:

> I have a secret garden
> Made from butterfly wings,
> A garden of color that sings.
> I walk there often, usually alone,
> Like most things I do,
> But sometimes I find myself walking
> With someone like you.

Nugget was denied any further chance to discuss Fran. A deep-seated rumbling started up. At first it seemed the Japanese were staging a surprise attack by setting off buried land mines. Until Rod, Nugget, and others found themselves standing on very shaky ground. Tent-flys collapsed, mess tins fell off trees, washing swung on lines, part of a ridge slid down a slope, jungle giants swayed and crashed. Someone yelled: "Earthquake!"

This was nothing extraordinary; New Guinea, like the islands of Japan, was earthquake-prone territory. Few members of the Australian force had ever experienced real quakes, but most of the Japanese had, so this was an instance of Nature unwittingly giving the advantage to the enemy. And being the nimble improvisers that they were, the Japanese seized on the disruption caused by the quake and attacked, forcing Rod's unit to retreat.

—————

Rod celebrated his seventeenth birthday by helping his unit to regain its former position, then advance until halted by a Japanese stand on a feature called Humpback Knoll, a smaller knoll set on top of the larger one, another natural fortress, with a commanding outlook in all directions, and an open swamp on either side, but with some stands of bamboo and clumps of trees in the space between its lower level and the ridge behind which the Australian troops were poised. The plan of attack, as outlined by Exton, was to use the trees and bamboo as cover and to try to gain a foothold on the pedestal of the knoll, then dig in and hope for rain to aid them in an attempt to take the summit.

The unit was by now overdue for relief and rest, but almost to a man (there was no secret about at least two who were not imbued with the zeal of the majority) the company wanted to see the campaign through. They all realized that the Japanese would defend and attack more fanatically than ever. Captured documents continued to confirm that they had not given up hope of breaking back through to Wau, then on to Port Moresby to launch an offensive against the Australian mainland.

The company was addressed by the battalion's commanding officer on the significance of the coming battle for Humpback Knoll. If it fell, then Salamaua was as good as in the bag. The lieutenant-colonel disclosed an interesting item from a captured document. For the Japanese it was to be a critical operation. The Japanese general in command of the area had informed his troops that the Emperor had learned with great sadness of the loss of Mubo, and that the fate of the Empire itself could depend on the battle ahead. It was certainly true that Humpback Knoll was a fulcrum where the whole conflict lay in the balance.

On the day before the operation, which was to start on the verge of daybreak the next morning, the company commander, Captain Exton, was faced with a dilemma. Mail, whether good, bad, or indifferent, always had an unsettling effect on the troops. There could be no worse time for it to arrive than on the eve of an action. But arrive it did and the postal courier had been seen, chains on the wheels of his jeep to help get through the mud. Word spread; the men wanted their mail pronto; Exton had no chance to hold it back until after the attack.

Rod received another letter from his mother, wishing him many happy returns of his birthday (while making no mention of his age). She had been received into the Roman Catholic Church and would be marrying Hal Frobish in a month, which meant in some two weeks time—her letter had taken a fortnight to reach Rod. She and Hal would be renting a flat in Elizabeth Bay. They had chosen it partly because the second bedroom, which would be Rod's, had a marvelous harbor view, all the way to the heads in one direction. He would be able to lie in bed and see the ships coming and going, the ferries on their routes, and the yachts at play on weekends.

"Sounds great," Nugget said, after Rod had revealed the contents of the letter. "Nothin' from your two female fans, eh?"

"No," Rod said. "But then I haven't written to them."

"I suppose I could always drop a line to young Fran," Nugget mused. "What do you reckon?"

"That's up to you, mate."

This was exactly what Rod had been thinking of doing himself, especially after reading Fran's poem again and again, sending the letter through Horrie in the hope that he could forward it to her. It disturbed him to think that another possible source of conflict besides their differing attitudes toward the Japanese was arising between him and his mate. Nugget's view of the enemy remained as rigid as before, while Rod had continued to try to see the better side of the enemy people, despite the callous sinking of the hospital ship, the execution of the young American pilot, and reports of other enemy atrocities which had filtered through to them. On the other hand, Japanese prisoners were still being summarily shot for no real reason, and a bombardier had been found carrying a spare haversack crammed with the ears of Japanese soldiers and marines which he had cut off.

These issues aside, the future in Sydney seemed exciting. A room with a harbor view. Maybe he would never see either of the two *Queens* there again, but there would certainly be plenty of other big ships to view.

Later in the day, he left Nugget at their tent-fly and looked in on the other members of his section. It was a noisy scene,

due to the enthusiasm the commanding officer had expressed for giving the Japanese some of their own treatment
by launching the attack with plenty of sound effects. Empty
oil cans were being beaten with sticks; high-pitched whistles
tested; a dented bugle coaxed into giving forth discordant
blasts; a siren whined, one which once told native coconut
plantation workers when it was time to start and to stop;
from a sheet of tin shaped into a megaphone, a lusty-voiced
infantryman bellowed: "Little yellow bastards! *You* die for
Tojo!"

Rod left Larry Donald and Fred Mullen until last. He
was prepared for hostility, and received this in plenty from
Donald, if only in looks. As for Mullen, Rod was amazed
to see him wearing his full kit, including respirator, as if in
readiness to take part in an amphibious landing. If it was a
dress rehearsal of some sort for the next morning, Mullen
had it all wrong; specific instructions had been issued that
the troops were to carry minimum equipment and rations
so that they could concentrate on weapons and ammunition.

Donald swore obscenely and said, "Trust you to turn up
now! But at least you're in time to say cheerio to Fred."

"I'm pullin' out," Mullen said. "Got a medical certificate
sayin' I'm too old for further active service."

Rod was angered. "You picked a fine time to turn it in."

"He's done his share!" Donald said.

"By gum, I have!" Mullen repeated on his own behalf.
"Two world wars in a row."

Something mystified Rod. At any time in the past Mullen
had only to declare his real age and he would have been
given the necessary medical certificate. Why pick now to
turn it all in? The answer wasn't long in coming. Rod

reached out to take hold of the grenade hooked by its lever to the webbing on Mullen's chest. Mullen stepped back sharply, but a little unsteadily since he was so heavily encumbered. The undressed timber upright supporting the ridge pole of the tent-fly stopped him retreating any farther.

"What the bloody hell do you think you're doing!" Donald demanded of Rod.

"We need all the ammo we can lay hands on," Rod said. "Fred won't be needing this grenade." And with that he grasped the grenade and lifted it to free it from the webbing, only to have to use both hands to stop it from plummeting to the ground.

"It's like a lump of lead!" he exclaimed.

And then, from the tense looks of Donald and Mullen, and the weight of the little pineapple, identical in every detail to the No. 36M hand grenade, right down to its black paint, he understood why Mullen was pulling out and how they planned to smuggle their loot to the mainland. The grenade was solid gold, and the reason why Mullen sweated, and swayed a bit on his feet, was because he was loaded down with the metal. The sort of full kit he normally carried weighed sixty-five pounds, a big load for a small man like Fred Mullen at any time. His rifle looked a genuine .303, but the native souvenirs in a string bag, a wooden mask and a carved crocodile, weighed down Mullen's arm so much that Rod felt justified in assuming they were also gold.

In fact, capitalizing on their experience in civilian life in the dubious art of disguising motor vehicles and coins, they had filched paints from an ammunition repair unit—different colors were used to give shells and other death-dealing devices their distinctive markings—and rifled field hospital supplies for plaster of Paris to use in making casts.

Coming to an immediate decision, Rod said, "Before you pull out, Fred, you'll have to leave anything that's gold with the platoon commander."

"Pig's arse he will!" Donald spat, while Mullen seemed to be having some trouble in trying to stand upright and keep his balance; the discovery about what he was carrying seemed to have become an extra burden.

Rod was adamant. "You've known since we hit Wau that it was illegal to touch the stuff."

"Illegal be buggered!"

"Not doin' no harm," Mullen put in lamely.

"I'm giving you an order," Rod said.

Mullen looked to Donald for guidance, but his co-conspirator could only fume and glare at Rod. The sound effects being rehearsed for the Japanese at dawn filled the background with cacophony. A scrap of cloud loomed, nearly became the ghost of an enemy soldier, then settled for being that of a kangaroo, then dissipated.

"Big an' all as they are," Donald said, finding words to fit his fury, "there are times when you're too big for those bloody boots. Just keep your nose out of this."

"I've told Fred what he's got to do."

"What *you* want to do is the question! Stay on as McKenzie? Or leave as Murray—minus stripes, medal, the lot?"

"That's for you to decide," Rod told him. Then, addressing Mullen again, he said, "Are you going to carry out the order?"

Donald shook his head at Mullen who then shook his, which meant he also shook a solid gold rising sun, the badge on the left brim of his slouch hat, disguised as weathered bronze.

After his attempts to enlist, his training, his service in other parts of the island, his discovery of a mission and his dedication to seeing it through, Rod had finally reached a confrontation with his original deception; but he could do nothing about it other than to say, "If that's the case, I'll have to go to Pollock." He had been pushed past the point of compromise.

"Oh, no you don't!" Donald snapped, making a grab to stop Rod leaving, but Rod tossed the solid gold grenade at him, and it slipped through the soldier's hands, winding him. In his wake, Rod heard Donald gasping to Mullen, "Get goin' Fred, while you've got the chance."

The casualty rate among officers had been high. Red-headed Lieutenant Jerry Pollock, commissioned in the field, was, like other remaining officers, war-weary but determined to be in the operation to capture Humpback Knoll and command the approach to Salamaua. As he sat outside his tent-fly, checking his compass and other gear, he was red-eyed with exhaustion, a condition which Rod seemed to aggravate when he stated that he was sorry he had to inform his platoon commander that he was under legal age for military service.

Pollock, a tough man, a railway ganger foreman in civilian life, used to handling tough men, but noted for his patience in doing so, now felt that he was fully entitled to explode.

"Holy Mother! What goes on around here? First Fred Mullen decides he's just discovered he's too old for further active service—and now you're telling me you're too young!"

"I'm not trying to get out of further service," Rod hastened to say. "Anything but."

"Then why tell me?"

"If I didn't, someone else would."

"Who?" Pollock demanded, casting an irritated glance in the direction of the blasting bugle.

Not only did Rod feel he had become a fugitive forced into having to give himself up; now he was being asked to become an informer as well.

"It's to do with the gold. Someone's been filching it."

"Does this *someone* know you're underage?"

"Yes, sir."

"And would that someone be a combination of Privates Mullen and Donald?"

"Yes, sir," said Rod. Perhaps it wasn't so surprising that Pollock should be so quick to identify the pilferers. Most of the unit knew the pair were up to something, although they were treated more as harmless hard-cases, scavengers, not malingerers in the true sense.

"From what I've heard, this comes as no revelation," Pollock said. "I would much sooner you hadn't told me, because you're forcing me to do something about it. Report the matter to the company commander—no doubt he'll inform me that you've got to be taken out of the line immediately."

"Sir," Rod said, painfully aware of what he had exposed himself to, "until tomorrow's op is over, could this be just between the two of us?"

"You don't seem to realize what you're asking me to do, McKenzie. If I fail to take some action at once, I could find myself facing a court-martial. You should have thought of that."

"I had no choice. Fred Mullen is weighed down with the stuff. He's heading for Wau."

"We'll have him picked up before he gets too far." Pollock reached inside the shelter of his tent-fly and brought out his field telephone. "I don't want to lose you, McKenzie—certainly not at this stage—but you'll have to pack your kit and be ready to head back to base."

It was as if Rod had been told that he was being dishonorably discharged.

Before he could use the field telephone, Pollock winced as they felt the full force of a shrieking whistle. And then came other sounds. Contributions to the general discord—but from another source. Different whistles and whines, followed by detonations and eruptions of earth as mortar bombs and shells from mountain guns fell in and around the camp.

"Bloody Nips!" Pollock cried, preparing to use the field telephone for another reason. "I warned Exton that we could be overdoing it. They've twigged that we're mounting something."

The company sergeant-major bawled, "Stand to!"

"You'll have to stay, McKenzie," Pollock said. "We're going to need you." And then Pollock spoke on the field telephone to the .company commander, while Rod raced back to the tent-fly where Nugget was clamping on his webbing. Rod was already wearing his, with ammunition in the pouches. He grabbed up his rifle while Nugget took his Owen gun, and they headed for their positions on the ridge, looking across the gully to the base of Humpback Knoll.

Some of the Japanese had slipped down from the top of the knoll to the pedestal in readiness to attack in the wake of the mortar bombs and shells which were coming from the top of the knoll; but Exton had called for an urgent air strike, and before the Japanese could move forward any farther, American dive-bombers came in, making several runs before they silenced the mountain guns and mortars.

As the company settled down for the night, still intending to carry out the operation next morning as planned, sentries were posted while others slept, or cleaned their weapons, or quietly smoked, or yarned. Rod checked his rifle, then gave his boots a good rub with water-proofing.

He had told Nugget how Donald and Mullen had conspired to spirit their gold back to the mainland, and about his showdown with them, and how he had reported the matter to the platoon commander.

Now, when they saw Pollock making his way towards them, they both thought that here was the end of Rod's military career. Pollock paused to talk to other men; it was impossible to read from his expressionless face what decision he might be bringing. When he reached them, he still showed nothing of his thoughts, but simply announced what had transpired.

"I reported the matter of your age to the company commander, McKenzie. I am instructed to take no action. The decision is on his head. Should you want to pull out, you're free to do so."

With that he moved on, leaving Rod to say, "Like hell!" to Nugget who gave his mate a whack on the back to celebrate the good news.

Donald was nearby, just below the rim of the ridge, and he taunted Rod with a sly grin, to which his section leader reacted by saying, "I don't suppose there's any hope of Fred changing his mind and coming back to lend a hand?"

"No," Donald answered, never more cocksure. "Like I said, he's done his share. By now he could be in Wau an' taking off for Moresby, next stop home."

Alas, the veteran of Gallipoli, France, Papua, and New Guinea wasn't to get even as far as Mubo. He was found on a track, knifed in the back, his throat cut. Many items of his kit and equipment were noted as missing: his grenade and souvenirs; his signet ring; his bayonet, water-bottle, mess tins, knife, fork, and spoon, steel helmet, tins of bully beef rations, packs of emergency rations, field dressings, safety razor, soap, shaving brush, mouthpiece of respirator, heels of his boots; but the rising sun badge remained on his slouch hat.

It was thought at first that this could have been the work of those bearing allegiance to a different rising sun, but the area was no longer penetrated by Japanese patrols, and according to the natives it was entirely free of Japanese stragglers. Besides, the bootmarks found around Mullen's body were hobnailed in the Australian style and had obviously been on the feet of those who had been keeping watch on the secret activities of the former coiner and the former car thief, possibly from an ammunition dump or an ordnance stores depot. But the discovery of Fred Mullen's fate lay a little ahead in time; after the crucial battle about to take place.

16

In the camp below the ridge, short services and prayers were held by padres from headquarters. Rod had never belonged to any particular church, but his grandmother had taken him to the Church of England when he was staying with her, so he joined the twenty or so at the service held by the C. of E. padre. Nugget went with him.

Throughout the night, he and Nugget and others of his section and platoon, along with members of fellow platoons, took turns in manning the top of the ridge. After a stint in the early hours, Rod slipped down to the camp for some coffee from the cookhouse cauldron. Nugget was already there, eager to pass on a juicy rumor which he had picked up from an American patrol that had been and gone.

"The Yanks are building a sort of super weapon," he told Rod. "A fleet of a hundred aircraft carriers, each with a hundred bombers, and they're all goin' to take off together and belt the daylights outa Japan, from top to bottom, every city, town, and village, all at the same time, like as if the whole country was being hit with one mighty bomb. So we could be home for Christmas."

For once Rod's guard dropped. "I reckon that'd be a bit rough," he said.

"Rough? Nothin's too rough for the bastards!"

"It would mean hitting helpless people," Rod said, thinking of Hiroshi Ohara's demure, kimono-clad fiancée.

Nugget stared. "You're not goin' soft on the Nips, are ya?"

"That'd be the day," Rod said; but he still found himself impelled to stand by what he felt. "I reckon the Japanese deserve everything we can give them. But wiping out the lot of them, that's going too far."

Rod returned to the steaming cauldron for another mug of coffee, disturbed that his feelings had surfaced so far. And he was still very aware of that other simmering possibility of conflict between Nugget and himself. Fran King. He had kept thinking about her, the way he had once been preoccupied with Brenda, ever since receiving her letter and, more significantly, her poem. He had folded it and tucked it into his wallet where he carried the few pound and ten shillings notes he still had when he got back from the mainland; also the last letter received from his grandmother. He imagined himself walking with Fran in Ohara's little Garden of Eden, hand in hand, her delicate fingers enclosed in his big protective mitt. He had done nothing yet to discourage Nugget's idea of writing to Fran and looking her up once he was back home in Sydney; a painful situation could be developing. It had led him to recall several of his grandmother's sayings.

Despite having told him that a blind eye was a very handy thing for anyone to have, she had qualified this particular piece of wisdom by telling him there were some things which you could not ignore. Once when he was staying with her, one of her neighbors had made the old lady fighting mad by throwing weeds over her back fence. She had marched into battle, saying as she set out, "If there's something you need to have out with anyone, the sooner you do it, the less there is to fight or fret about in the long run."

Quite apart from the relevance of that, Rod felt the need to clarify the matter in his mind—and he decided he would have to be frank with Nugget, even show him Fran's poem. But that would have to wait until the imminent show was over.

With two hours to go before daybreak, rain began to sweep across the ranges. The weather report relayed from battalion headquarters was for alternating sunshine and rain. Dawn, as always in this latitude, would come swiftly; an hour before it was due, half the men slept while the other half were on the ridge, either at the rim or waiting just below it. At this stage there was a lull in the rain, and as the trees dripped, a highly-amplified voice broadcasting in the most impeccable English came from the lower level of Humpback Knoll. It began with a cry that all troops had come to loathe.

"Wakey, wakey! Wakey, wakey!" And as those on the top of the ridge armed their weapons and shrank down a little behind the rim, the voice continued: "And a very good morning to you, Aussies! Here is something for you to think about. It's being kept from you, alas. Your country is overrun with American troops—handsome, with plenty of money to spend, and your wives and girlfriends are surrendering to them in droves."

The loudspeaker seemed to be situated in a clump of trees on the lower pedestal of the knoll. Everyone on the lee slope of the ridge opposite was awake now, those along its rim being joined by others. Unable to restrain themselves, some of the Australians opened up in the general direction of the loudspeaker with submachine guns and rifles, only to be answered by maddeningly polite laughter.

"It's all too true, I fear," the voice went on in the same cultured tones. "Your women are being stolen from you."

Someone on the ridge aimed a torch beam at the source of the voice and drew bursts of enemy submachine-gun fire. Jeering laughter came from the loudspeaker, and a low angry growl ran along the top of the Australian ridge, where the men were incensed almost to the point of precipitate action, to get at the loudspeaker and the owner of that infuriatingly cultured voice. But Exton and Pollock were on hand to restrain them. The company commander had no doubt that the enemy tactic was to try to lure his men down the front face of the ridge and forward in the darkness. So he ordered them to hold all fire and ignore the taunts.

It put a great strain on the men, nevertheless, as they were baited again and again, their only respite being when the rain came down so heavily that the loudspeaker could not be heard.

As day began to break, Exton used his binoculars to try to narrow down the point where the loudspeaker was placed in the clump of trees. He spotted nothing until the light strengthened, then he saw wires hanging parallel to a tree trunk, and through the leaves higher up discerned a roundish shape. That this was indeed the loudspeaker was confirmed when further taunts issued from it, so he called on two of the unit's marksmen to come to his side—Lance Corporal McKenzie and another from a different platoon.

Rod and his fellow marksman took up their positions and waited for another round of taunting; this time the Oxford-accented voice claimed that half of the women in Australia had been infected with venereal disease by their dissolute, over-sexed American allies. The two marksmen opened up, firing their shots one by one and silencing the amplified voice in mid-sentence.

The time for the planned attack came, but Exton held back. He had decided to have the ground between the front of their ridge and Humpback Knoll checked, so he waited for a heavy shower to give cover to those going out to reconnoiter the area. The unit's booby-trap expert was among them, a watchmaker in civilian life. He found trip-wires connected to grenades and clusters of high-explosive sticks, as well as buried mines. He did nothing about the latter, except to mark their positions, while cutting the wires of the booby-traps.

Before the shower eased, the probing party had returned to the ridge, the ground between it and the lower level of the knoll cleared of booby-traps, and paths through the mines marked with sticks.

All was set for the attack, except cover—and Exton waited for another downpour.

Though early morning still, the sun, when it appeared, was blisteringly hot. With it certain creatures of the area also came out, among the butterflies a rich blue and violet specimen indulging in its first free flight, sailing and gliding, swooping and looping, catching Rod's eye as it crossed the no-man's-land between the ridge and the knoll. Someone who made pictures from butterfly wings would have been able to use parts of it for seas or skies, distant hills and mountains, lakes and lagoons, or even fields of larkspurs, like the ones his grandmother had grown in her garden.

The attack was launched in the middle of a deluge, the Australians sliding down the forward face of the ridge and crossing to the lower level of the knoll where some of the fighting was bayonet to bayonet, the battle seesawing with the rain and sunshine, the Australians withdrawing into stands of thick bamboo—although the Japanese brought in a heavy machine gun to cut down the bamboo and deny the attackers its cover during the sunny breaks, going through it like a chainsaw.

Casualties began to mount on either side, many dead, many wounded. As Rod and Nugget kept close to each other, Larry Donald, as a member of the section, was obliged to stay with them, although he kept well behind them, blatantly using them as shields. But in the way that things go in battle, a burst of submachine-gun fire aimed at Rod and Nugget missed both of them and passed in the narrow gap between them to strike Donald, killing him outright. He never knew of Fred Mullen's fate. Their deaths meant that a certain question remained unanswered: had they obtained the gold by assiduous digging and panning, or stumbled on a hoard buried by residents who had evacuated in the face of the invading Japanese?

Several times, the Australians took over weapon-pits on the lower pedestal, either killing their occupants or forcing them to pull back up to the summit of the knoll. The conflict seemed to be going in favor of the Australians when the heavy rain suddenly stopped, leaving the attackers badly exposed in blazing sunlight. But only momentarily.

It was at this critical point that nature played a dramatic part. The defenders of Humpback Knoll, by digging foxholes and weapon-pits along the lower pedestal level, had interfered with its natural matrix and allowed the rainwater to penetrate the ground, the result being a landslide which left a group of twenty Japanese without cover and no hope of escaping the hail of Australian fire which cut them down as surely as their heavy machine guns had dealt with the thick stems of bamboo.

Surging forward, Rod and Nugget in the leading sections, the attackers took over enemy positions and began to consolidate in readiness to mount an assault on the summit of the knoll, hoping to occupy it and open the way to Salamaua.

But ammunition had run short. Rod had fired his last round. Fresh supplies were on the way, but as the two native carriers bringing them reached the base of the pedestal, another great slab of earth and mud broke free, rolling down over the two carriers, burying them and their ammunition.

Some infantrymen carried small shovel-shaped tools for digging weapon-pits and slit trenches; they hastened to put them to work to extricate the buried carriers and retrieve the ammunition. Other helpers used bare hands.

Rod waited anxiously, keeping well down in the captured weapon-pit, Nugget beside him, all magazines for his Owen gun empty. Glancing up, Rod saw a bush starting to move backward about halfway up the slope. He realized the bush was being used as camouflage by a Japanese soldier. Nugget had commented, when they first saw the force they were up against, "These Japs are big buggers." And they were, some six feet in height. But the one using the bush turned out to be much smaller, and he abandoned his camouflage once it was apparent the moving bush had been spotted. As he started grinding alone up the slope, a stocky, bandy-legged figure, sword scabbard trailing, Rod recognized him. It was Captain Astashi.

"That's the bloke who beheaded the Yank pilot!" Nugget exclaimed.

"I know," Rod said. And with his bayonet fixed on his rifle, despite a cry of caution from his mate, Rod took off up the slope.

The bayonet glinted in the brilliant sunshine that had

followed the last rain shower, and a flash from it registered in the corner of Astashi's eye; still climbing, he half-turned, and saw the hulking Australian ascending, the very soldier who had left the giant bootmarks.

Astashi fumbled at his side to grip and draw his pistol from its holster; Rod's impetus was such that Astashi had only moments to aim and fire. That is, if Rod hadn't balked and stumbled. And what caused him to balk was what seemed to him to be a firework with a piercing blue flame, spinning close to his eyes: a blue and violet butterfly gamboling deliriously with a female in an ecstatic whirl of giddy courtship flight.

He had to drop a hand to the ground to steady himself before propelling himself upward once more, but he had granted his adversary the precious moments needed to draw his pistol, aim and fire.

The bullet struck Rod in the side. And now, as he labored to reach the executioner, his boots became so heavy that they might have been cast in illicit gold. Even so, with his momentum fading away, he managed to keep on and drive the shaft of steel fitted to the end of his rifle into Astashi's body. It was not a simple act of vengeance for the beheading of the young American pilot; it was because of Astashi's desecration of human dignity, something which Rod was determined to believe so many of the Japanese race must possess.

Astashi screamed, but before he threw his arms up and fell, he discharged the pistol again—and Rod took this bullet in his chest. He lost his hold on his rifle. The bayonet remained thrust into Astashi as he fell, kicking violently on his back, then going limp.

Rod swayed, his knees buckling as he sank to the ground. Another belt of rain swept across the slope of the knoll, obscuring the view of those at the lower level, where Nugget remained stunned by his mate's impulsive pursuit of the bush that had become a man and by the glimpse he'd had of what had ensued. He was beside himself with dread, raging to bring back his mate, alone if need be. But others were boiling to go with him.

A rescue attempt was put to Lieutenant Pollock who referred it to the company commander. Captain Exton well understood Nugget's distress and respected his readiness to go forward, but at first he said no—not yet. He wanted to get a spotter plane overhead to try to give him some estimate of the numbers and deployment of the enemy on the summit of Humpback Knoll. But then, when the rain eased, two Japanese were seen racing back to the summit from the point where Astashi and Rod had fallen; since they were not carrying anyone, it appeared that they had left the fallen Captain where he lay, presumably dead. The spotter plane couldn't operate just yet, so Exton gave Nugget the go-ahead.

With two other infantrymen, Nugget waited through a stifling break of sunshine for the next shower, a dense dark blanket of rain that gave plenty of cover as they crept up the slope of the knoll, to find Rod stretched out on his back under the broad leaves, beside the dead Astashi, and Rod's rifle, no longer embedded in the officer, lying to one side.

At a gentle touch from Nugget, one which he did not really expect would bring any response, Rod's eyes slowly opened, at first misty and not focusing; then they seemed to sharpen, and he managed a grin as he recognized his mate. His jungle-green shirt had been soaked with blood, but only the stains remained, the rest washed away by the rain. As Nugget and the others slipped their hands under him to carry him, Rod shut his eyes tight and clenched his teeth in the face of pain.

Down below the pedestal of the knoll, where trees offered a measure of shelter, Nugget and the two infantrymen carefully lowered Rod onto a ground-sheet as the M.O., Captain Boyle, waited. It took Boyle little time to reach a verdict. He stood up, shaking his head to Exton and Pollock, while Nugget was close enough to hear what he had to say.

"His spine's shattered. Afraid it won't be long."

As the M.O. gave the stricken young jungle fighter an injection which might make his passing less agonizing, Nugget knelt at Rod's side, and it was only now that he saw that his mate was wearing only socks on his feet.

"Where's his boots?" Nugget wanted to know.

One of the infantrymen who had helped carry him down said: "He didn't have any—not when we picked him up."

Despite the drone of the rain, pouring like glassy shingle off the sheltering leaves, Rod managed to be heard.

"Souvenired . . ." he murmured.

"Whadda ya say, mate?" Nugget was quick to ask as he lowered an ear.

"Couple of Japs . . . came down t'make sure Astashi was finished . . . one took m'wallet . . . the other m'boots . . ."

"Souvenired ya bloody boots! The bastard! The low thievin' yella bastard! Souveniring ya bloody boots!"

"Don't reckon I'll be needing 'em," Rod murmured, calmly resigned. He had seen enough of death, and of men dying, to know his own situation, and he went on to whisper one of his grandmother's sayings: "When your time's come . . ."

"Gee, mate," Nugget whispered, holding Rod's hand in both of his, feeling the ominous coldness.

It became a struggle for Rod to breathe, but his vision

seemed to increase, not to see what was around him, but things not visible to his companions. Something special seemed to fascinate him, and between gasps he managed to say, "How about that? The two of them . . . the two *Queens* . . . in the harbor . . ."

It was the vision of one who was still a boy at heart even if he was also a seasoned warrior.

"Butterflies . . ." Rod said. "Swarms . . ." And his eyes moved as he followed what others could not see. Presently they became still, and after a little he murmured, smiling, "It's just like the picture . . ."

"What picture's that, mate?"

"The little Jap's . . ."

Nugget hadn't seen it, of course, but Rod had described it to him—and he knew that he had given it to Fran King.

After this, Rod did not try to speak again; but it was apparent from the expression in his eyes that he was entranced by whatever scene or vision filled them. And with the smile still on his lips, the light in his eyes faded away.

Captain Boyle made the final pronouncement. Captain Exton would have instructed the burial to take place there and then, as was the practice; but the rain continued to fall so heavily that any grave would have filled with water before it could be fully excavated. And so the burial had to wait.

The rain persisted throughout the rest of the day, as did Nugget's outrage at the theft of his mate's special boots.

The unit had dug in on the lower pedestal level of Humpback Knoll, avoiding places where there might be further landslides. A spotter plane had not been able to operate, so the remaining enemy strength could only be estimated, based on the number of dead counted and the probable wounded. The opposing forces would still be evenly matched, unless the Japanese managed to bring in reinforcements—it was up to the American regiment on the Australian flank to ensure that this did not happen. No further plan of attack had yet been forthcoming from the company commander; it was essential to reconnoiter the summit of the knoll from the air first, and with the rain set in it could mean a wait of days.

Once darkness fell, the rain became spasmodic again, the light of a half-moon breaking fitfully through fast-moving clouds. During these intervals, the summit of the knoll loomed above, and observers claimed that from what they were able to glimpse it was strongly cordoned.

At the coffee cauldron many besides Nugget grieved for lost comrades; and it became apparent, as the lower ranks quietly talked to one another, that one loss stood out against all the others—Rod McKenzie's boots. It was a craven act, in a way worse than the taking of a man's life. It was as if part of the man's very soul had been stolen. A notion grew in Nugget's mind: he would slip away, creep up the slope of the knoll to the summit, find a gap in the cordon of troops ringing it, locate the stolen boots, and bring them back. There would be no point in letting his platoon or company commander know his plan; each would be certain to quash the idea. He could not restrain himself from mentioning it at the coffee cauldron to those who kept sympathizing with him and expressing their anger at the souveniring of the boots. He found many ready to go with him.

Nugget believed that only a very small party of men could get through the summit cordon—and if they were discovered, there would be no chance of escape. So there was no point in taking rifles or submachine guns, which would only encumber them as they climbed. When he saw that the unit's booby-trap expert and its crack unarmed combat exponent were among the volunteers, he had his team—just the three of them.

They set out, all wearing dark berets, their faces, ears, necks, throats, arms and hands well covered with blacking. They waited for a heavy fall of rain and ascended under its pall, three creeping shadows. They paused short of the cordon of sentries in weapon-pits, and then, when the rain became a deluge, they crawled—almost swam—through a virtual wall of water until they were within the enemy camp, very faint illumination coming from the mouths of foxholes and entrances to bunkers.

From what appeared to be the central bunker came sounds of inebriation—chattering and giggling. This, in fact, was thanks to the action of Australian Rod McKenzie in disposing of Captain Astashi. With that officer's departure some of the rigid discipline he had imposed on his men had gone. The handful of his surviving officers, together with an English-speaking intelligence officer, were in the late commander's bunker, liberally indulging themselves in the captain's private store of a potent brand of sake. The intelligence officer had been posted to this unit to examine any captured documents, since the Japanese were confused by the Allied strategy. In Japanese, he was regaling the other officers with snippets read from letters found on the bodies of fallen Aussies, ridiculing endearments received from wives and girlfriends.

Nugget saw that the booby-trap expert was tempted to toss just one of the grenades he carried into the bunker. That would certainly dispose of all its occupants; but it would also invite disaster. So they continued their search. Another bunker was found to be an ammunition store, crammed with a range and quantity that would ensure the defenders could hold out for weeks.

The three passed on, finding several foxholes quietly occupied by sleeping men; and then one where a solitary soldier sat on his haunches, a tiny flame burning from a wick floating in a small shallow bowl of oil, using a penknife as he seemed to scrape mud from one of the souvenired boots. The next move was left to the unarmed combat expert who, like a professional hangman, took pride in the finesse with which he could dispatch a human being. Swiftly and soundlessly he overpowered and strangled the Japanese soldier, leaving Nugget free to take the two souvenired boots.

Before the three intruders withdrew, there was something the booby-trap expert insisted was too good an opportunity to miss. He went to work with his particular expertise with fuses and detonators, linking together boxes and stacks of the Japanese ammunition. When the first lot went up, the booby-trap expert trusted the rest would go. He set a time delay one hour ahead to trigger it all.

With the rain providing sweeping curtains to screen their return, the three slipped through the cordon of sentries.

Thus were McKenzie's boots retrieved.

One hour later, when the ammunition store on the summit of the knoll erupted, the blast, though immense, was still deadened by the rain. Captain Exton, Lieutenant Pollock, and other officers and men not in the know about what had been happening, were deeply mystified. But there was a quiet air of triumph among those gathered around the camp coffee cauldron.

In the morning, the weather lifted long enough for a spotter plane to be brought overhead, and a report was relayed to Exton that there was no sign of a single Japanese soldier or marine on the summit of the knoll except those who lay dead around the edge of a great gaping hole.

A probe was sent up to investigate, one which Nugget

Bates made sure he joined. Those who had not been killed in the blast had fled. So Humpback Knoll fell into Australian hands and the way to the isthmus of Salamaua, which could be glimpsed ahead, was open.

As for the souvenired boots, they were now openly shown to be in Nugget's possession. He accounted for this by claiming that he had found them in a vacated foxhole on the knoll, although he very nearly gave himself away when examining them for the first time in daylight. To his fury, the toe cap of each boot appeared to have been mutilated.

"Look at that!" he fumed. "The bloody Jap wasn't satisfied with thievin' the boots, he had to bloody well vandalize them!"

Their temporary owner had not been using the penknife to remove mud from the boots after all, but to deface them with some Japanese characters.

"Get them back onto McKenzie's feet," Captain Exton told Nugget, "and we'll go ahead with the burial."

But Rod was not buried wearing these boots, his last and largest pair. Nugget decided they belonged elsewhere, and he swapped them with those which his mate had been wearing when he arrived back from Sydney and had carried in his pack in case of emergency. And so young Corporal Rodney Murray, M.M. (served as McKenzie), enlisted aged fifteen, died of wounds aged just seventeen, was laid to rest.

17

With items of his own gear stuffed into them and around them, Nugget Bates carried Rod's boots in his pack through the shambles of Salamaua, through the wreckage of another Japanese stronghold at Lae, through the high kunai grass in the Ramu Valley and across its skeins of rivers, then along the razor-back of Shaggy Ridge.

Since Rod's real name, next-of-kin, and home address had become known to his company commander, his mother was notified of his death through official channels. Nugget wrote to her, and to Horrie, and to Brenda and Fran King, telling them that Rod had died peacefully and about the action in which he had been fatally wounded. He heard back eventually from everyone, except that Brenda replied on behalf of the King family without making any mention of Fran.

It was nearly six months later that Nugget came to Sydney on a long leave.

In the suburb of Padstow where he had grown up the Bates clan gathered for his welcome home, and to celebrate the fact that he had been mentioned in dispatches for his part in holding a dugout on Shaggy Ridge. This entitled him to wear a small bronze oak leaf on his chest. It was a minor award, but to his immediate family, and to his aunts, uncles, cousins, and others, it was as if he had won the Victoria Cross. The truth was that he had stayed put simply because he was determined not to be parted from his pack and its hobnailed contents.

The next day, Sunday, he woke with a pulsating hangover, but it did not lessen his awareness that he had a sacred duty to carry out. It was a sultry morning in early February as he rode out on his Norton motorbike. He had organized some gasoline coupons at the leave and transit depot. He had a good fast run with so little traffic on the roads, and the air helped clear his head.

He wore plain lightweight khaki shirt and trousers, somehow feeling half-naked in them after wearing jungle-greens for so long. He had emptied his pack of everything except the boots which he had cleaned for this day; he had applied brown polish thickly to the toe caps to try to cover up the ugliness of the cuts and slashes on them.

He reached Ultimo and set about locating the street in which Rod had lived, then the cottage with its door still looking newly-painted. Another family was in residence. He passed the horse-trough where two small boys sat in the rubbish and rubble, using wood slats and imagining themselves paddling a concrete canoe.

Having gleaned quite a bit about Rod's home territory from his mate, he was able to find his way to the street where the Kings lived. He stopped outside their cottage, propped up his machine, and then rang the front door bell.

As he waited, he began to perspire, more from apprehension than the closeness of the morning. He had tried to rehearse what to say, but didn't know who would greet him—Brenda, her mother, perhaps Fran, or even the major. And while his purpose in coming here centered on Brenda, he hoped it might lead to a meeting with Fran.

It was Brenda who opened the door, looking both puzzled and wary, realizing from the burnished atebrin-yellow of his skin that he was very recently from the islands. She was a good looker, all right, he thought. Could be twenty or even more, allowing for a certain air of unsureness about herself. Yet since she was almost Rod's age, Nugget knew she wasn't yet eighteen.

Once he had introduced himself, she knew immediately who he was. "It was good of you to write to us about Rod," she said.

"Thanks for your letter, too," Nugget said as he slipped off his pack and started to unfasten the brass buckles.

Brenda watched with increased wariness as he opened the pack and extracted of all things two massive brown army boots. She realized instantly what they were and stepped back, distancing herself from them, with an inborn fear of anything which had belonged to the dead.

"Rod was wearing these boots when he went into action for the last time," Nugget told her as he held a boot in each hand, leaving the pack at his feet. "They were souvenired by a Jap, but we got 'em back." He brought the toe caps close to each other. "The Jap cut them about, probably scrawlin' his name on 'em, but what else would you expect—flamin' vandals."

It was only now that he was aware of the effect the boots were having on her. She had gripped her hands tightly, but couldn't stop herself from trembling. Tears welled in her eyes and she whispered, "Poor Rod."

Such a heartfelt response confirmed what Nugget had been convinced about: that Brenda would readily accept his offer, so he said, "Knowing the way he felt about you, I thought you'd like to have them."

"These boots?" she said, edging farther back.

"Yeah." But as he held them out to her she retreated again, saying, "No, no. I couldn't possibly." She started to weep. "I was always so unkind to him."

With this came a flood of tears, and she turned and ran down the passageway, suddenly more a child than an adult, calling to her mother who was in the kitchen.

Very much the mother hen, Helen King reached the door, demanding, "Who *are* you—and what is it you want?"

Abject at the way things had gone, Nugget identified himself a second time. Helen King hastened to change her attitude. The boots were treasured keepsakes, she realized that. And the New Guinea veteran had come here with the very best of intentions.

"I'm sure Brenda respects your offer," she tried to assure him. "Believe me, she was deeply distressed when the terrible news came through. Weren't we all? But these boots would be out of place here. What about his battalion? Or his mother? She's moved from near here. I'm afraid I don't know her new address."

"I've got it, thanks," Nugget said.

"I would strongly suggest you take the boots to her."

It hadn't occurred to Nugget that Brenda would refuse the boots, and he simply hadn't thought of anyone else.

Helen King's hand was on the door handle. "I would like to ask you in, but knowing how Brenda must be feeling, I think it would be better if I didn't. You do understand?"

"Sorry to have upset her."

"You were only doing what you thought was best," she said as he started to return the boots to his pack. "It was a very fine thought."

She waited for him to go; but he couldn't leave without asking about the person who had been so often in his thoughts, even if her image had been obtained only through Rod.

"How is Fran getting along?" he asked. It was clumsy and blunt, but he didn't know how else to go about it.

Helen King stiffened at what she took to be a liberty, but then, maintaining her placatory attitude, she said, "Oh, like the rest of us, she's been having her problems."

Then she closed the door, and presumably went to console the daughter she doted on.

Back beside his Norton, Nugget pondered what to do now. Since he was so close to the Benson home, he could call on Horrie, but he knew the milk carter would be asleep at this hour, so he decided to leave that visit until another time and to make his way to Elizabeth Bay. Not that he had decided to present Rod's boots to the newly-wed Mrs. Hal Frobish; rather to meet her first and then gauge whether she was a fit recipient.

The motorbike started up explosively, and when it moved off Nugget rode not only the machine but a racket that seemed strong enough to fracture road surfaces. As he roared through Surry Hills, it occurred to him that this was where the milk and ice depot was located. Maybe someone there could solve another problem for him—how to get hold of Fran King's Land Army address so that he could try to get in touch with her.

He knew he was getting closer to the depot when he overtook a rumbling dray hauled by a hairy, thickset horse, with a grizzled driver wearing a rubber apron. On the flat top of the dray, half-covered with sodden sacks, were a few blocks of ice with their edges and corners melting. Trickles of water from the dray left parallel lines of damp along the street. The driver glowered at him as Nugget cut back his speed to be able to follow the dray, which began to move faster as the horse tried to keep ahead of the uproar made by Nugget's pride and joy, which had been on stocks since he had joined up.

Horse and dray turned another corner, and as they swung off the road and under a high archway, Nugget pulled up. On an arc at the top of the arch was the name of the milk and ice depot. He parked his machine and looked into the yard: offices, cool-rooms, and other buildings one side; stables the other, with two-wheeled carts and four-wheeled drays drawn up in lines between them.

The driver of the dray headed toward the cashier's office, scowling at the soldier as he crossed the yard, leaving a slightly-built stable-girl to attend to his horse.

Maybe this stable-girl could answer his query, Nugget thought. As she released the horse from between the shafts of the dray, he stepped into the yard. She wore gum boots, gray riding-breeches, and a white blouse. Her hair was medium brown, gold strands catching the light as she moved about. Hearing his boots on the asphalt, she looked up.

Confronted by the stable-girl's friendly eyes and smile, Nugget said, "Excuse me. I was wondering if you could help me? It's about someone who used to work here."

The request obviously alarmed her. "If you mean Rod Murray," she said, assuming he was looking for an army friend, "I'm sorry. I'm afraid . . ."

"I know all about Rod," Nugget said. "I was a friend of his."

"You were!"

He nodded. "Well, yeah, I reckon it'd be fair t'say, I was his best friend. His mate."

The girl's face lit up after the shadow her alarm had cast over it. "You wouldn't be Nugget Bates, would you?"

He gasped in surprise. "Matter of fact, I am."

"Rod told me all about you. Boy, do you have nightmares!"

"Rod told you?" And then, it was Nugget's turn to divine to whom he was speaking. "You must be . . ."

"Fran," she said for him. "Fran King."

"I thought you were in the Land Army."

"You thought right," she said. "Sad to tell," she went on with a rueful air, "they found out how old I was. So I'm back working here—much to the delight of my dear mother and darling sister."

Nugget grinned and Fran laughed, then asked, "Anyway, who is the someone who used to work here?"

"Need you ask?" he said shyly.

"Perhaps I can guess," she said, shy too.

As he told her how he had spoken to Rod about looking her up or even writing to her, she remembered how Rod had said his best friend was only half his size; but that made him more *her* size. And he was nice, too. He told her how he had called at her home and seen Brenda and her mother, and what had happened about the boots which he and two others had rescued.

"Would you mind if I saw them?" she asked quietly.

He slipped off the pack again, and as he unfastened the buckles, Fran stroked the horse to pacify him and told him to be patient; she would feed and water him presently.

Nugget had no fear that Fran would become hysterical or break down, as her sister had done. But her eyes were moist as she took one of the boots from him.

"Brenda should have accepted them," she said. "Rod

would have wanted her to have them, the way he felt about her."

Suddenly Nugget thought he had the answer. "Why don't *you* have them?"

She gave it a moment's thought, then shook her head. "Imagine Mum and Brenda allowing them in the house! That little butterfly picture Rod gave me, I'd like to frame it, but they wouldn't stand for that. So I carry it around with me."

"Always?" he asked.

Fran returned the boot to him, and from a pocket of her riding-breeches she produced a purse, and drew out the square of white silk, then revealed the treasure it enfolded.

Nugget whistled at the instant brilliance. "I've often wondered what it looked like," he said. And then he was quiet, overcome by a certain reverence, for here, even though it had been made by a Japanese soldier, was the original of the scene that had apparently been the last image in his mate's eyes, the azure sky beyond the purple mountains through which Rod had started out on his journey into the unknown. Perhaps, as Rod had once seemed to hint, there could be one or two Japanese who might not be as bad as most of them.

After returning the scene to her purse, alongside a copy of the poem she had sent to Rod, she said to Nugget, "If anyone should have the boots, it's you."

"We could always go fifty-fifty," he mused.

"One each?" she said with a startled little laugh.

"He'd approve, I'm sure." He decided to take the boots home for his mother to look after. Then he asked Fran, "How do you like parties?"

"Oh, I'm a real party girl."

"My mob—that's my family—they're running another

tonight. For those who couldn't make it to the one last night. Which means they'll all be there again anyway. You'd be very welcome."

The horse had decided he had been kept waiting for far too long and started to head for his stable on his own, so Fran had to go with him. "I'd love to come," she said.

"I could pick you up—as long as you don't mind riding on the back of a motorbike."

"Next to horses," she called, stumbling along beside the horse, "I'm crazy about motorbikes."

"See you about seven. You'll hear me arriving."

And, indeed, so did half of Ultimo.

That night, the two boots were on show, everyone at the party marveling at them, not only because of their extraordinary size but also because of where they had been and the heroic deeds of the young man who had worn them. It was as if Rod himself were present as the guest of honor. And, as Nugget pointed out, if any proof was needed that the Japanese were barbarians, there was the evidence on the toe caps of the boots.

Epilogue

Two hours after the roll-on, roll-off Japanese freighter had berthed at Darling Harbor, a party of those who had occupied its limited passenger accommodation arrived at the Cremorne Point home of Nelson James (Nugget) Bates. A vice-president of the motor vehicle manufacturer who owned the ship, another senior executive, and their wives. Already arrived at the house were Sydney-based business associates, including the managing director of Nugget's advertising agents, and the producer who made his television ads at a film studio in Surry Hills, once a milk and ice depot.

After having served for a short time before his discharge from the Second AIF with occupation forces in Japan, Nugget had come to appreciate its people. Besides, his attitude toward them had been influenced by his wife Fran, seven years his junior, and still youthful-looking. It was apparent they were a devoted couple, as they served drinks on the patio overlooking the magnificent harbor, which had never seen passenger liners to match in size and grandeur the legendary sisters who had last anchored here decades ago, the *Queen Mary* and the *Queen Elizabeth*.

Inside the house, moving toward the dinner table, the Japanese visitors were intrigued by the trophies—cups, shields, testimonials awarded to their host. But what attracted their attention more than anything else was the curious sight of a glass case containing a pair of big brown boots. The Australian guests knew the story behind them, and it was obvious that the Japanese guests would like to share it.

For fear of questions being asked which could lead to some embarrassment, Nugget and Fran had debated whether to remove the boots for the night. But Fran had been confident that between them, she and her husband could handle any awkward questions with diplomacy. And so the story about them and the youth who had worn them was briefly told once again.

The wife of the vice-president remained fascinated by them, and kept closely studying the scoring on the toe caps, even when Fran tried to divert her attention to the small framed picture which had been made from butterfly wings by one of their own soldiers in New Guinea.

When the wife finally turned away from the glass case, her comment about the boots astonished her host and hostess.

"That is a very fine inscription," she said.

"Inscription?" Nugget said.

"On the boots," said the Japanese wife.

Seeing the looks of consternation exchanged between Nugget and Fran, the vice-president explained, "My wife is a student of our language in all its forms. She lectures at the university." And then he left it to her to reveal to Nugget and Fran that the inscription was the work of someone with elementary writing skills.

Reading from one toe cap and then the other, she translated what the inscriber, another Japanese soldier, had recorded: *These boots were taken from the feet of an Australian hero.*